"I'm no fairy-tale prince, Ren.

"I'm not sweet or gentle. And I'm no one's knight in shining armor. You are gorgeous. An amazing, accomplished woman. An incredible mother. I'm not the man you deserve."

"But you're the man I want. Tonight." She shivered beneath his intense stare. Her fingers trembled as she touched the heated skin along his collarbone.

He sucked in a quiet breath, his piercing gaze still locked with hers. But he made no move to block her or draw her in closer. He was testing her. Maybe he needed to be sure that she was serious. That this was really what she wanted.

It was.

Renee lifted onto her toes, her eyes drifting closed as she pressed a kiss to his chest. Then another to his shoulder. Then another to his neck.

Cole wrapped his arms around her waist, hauling her body against him.

This time, there was no hesitation.

* * *

The Bad Boy Experiment by Reese Ryan
is part of The Bourbon Brothers series.

Dear Reader,

Welcome back to Magnolia Lake, Tennessee—home of the King's Finest Distillery and the wealthy Abbott family. In *The Bad Boy Experiment*, we finally get youngest son and family rebel Cole Abbott's story. Cole has been a reader favorite since he first appeared in *Engaging the Enemy*. I'm thrilled to introduce you to the woman who steals this bad boy's heart.

When Cole's high school crush—brilliant scientist and divorced single mom Renee Lockwood—returns to town, it turns the successful real estate developer's world upside down. As they both vie for the same land and become unwilling next-door neighbors, things heat up. Ren proposes a no-strings fling. But for Cole, it quickly becomes much more. Can he convince the skittish divorcée he's ready to settle down and that their love is worth the risk?

Thank you for joining me for the passion, secrets and drama of my Bourbon Brothers series. Got a question or comment? Visit reeseryan.com/desirereaders. While there, join my VIP Readers newsletter list for book news, giveaways and more.

Until our next adventure in Magnolia Lake,

Reese Ryan

REESE RYAN

THE BAD BOY EXPERIMENT

ISBN-13: 978-1-335-73538-6

The Bad Boy Experiment

This edition published by arrangement with Harlequin Books S.A.

For questions and comments about the quality of this book, please contact us at CustomerService@Harlequin.com.

Harlequin Enterprises ULC
22 Adelaide St. West, 41st Floor
Toronto, Ontario M5H 4E3, Canada
www.Harlequin.com

Printed in U.S.A.

Reese Ryan writes sexy, emotional love stories served with a heaping side of family drama.

Reese is a native Ohioan with deep Tennessee roots. She endured many long, hot car trips to family reunions in Memphis via a tiny clown car loaded with cousins.

Connect with Reese via Facebook, Twitter, Instagram, TikTok or reeseryan.com. Join her VIP Readers Lounge at bit.ly/VIPReadersLounge. Check out her YouTube show, where she chats with fellow authors, at bit.ly/ReeseRyanChannel.

Books by Reese Ryan

Harlequin Desire

The Bourbon Brothers

Savannah's Secret
The Billionaire's Legacy
Engaging the Enemy
A Reunion of Rivals
Waking Up Married
The Bad Boy Experiment

Visit her Author Profile page at Harlequin.com, or reeseryan.com, for more titles.

You can find Reese Ryan on Facebook, along with other Harlequin Desire authors, at Facebook.com/harlequindesireauthors!

For my son, Jay, and my two grandsons, Dimples and Bam Bam. I love you to pieces. You inspire me every day, and my world is so much better for having all of you in it.

To all of my incredible readers: your enthusiasm for this series has been truly touching. I'm thrilled that you've enjoyed the romantic adventures of the Abbotts and their extended family as much as I have. Thank you for being an integral part of my journey.

To Brenda Jackson, Beverly Jenkins, Rochelle Alers and Donna Hill: thank you so much for blazing trails and lighting the way. And thank you for your encouragement, advice and support.

Thank you to my writing bestie, K. Sterling, for always being there for early-morning and late-night writing sprints. Thank you, Katee Robert, for being so generous with your knowledge and experience. And thank you to Tasha L. Harrison and the entire Wordmakers community for making the hard days feel easier. Love y'all! Sorry for those extra gray hairs.

To the Harlequin Desire team: thank you for all you've done to give a home to, create, refine and promote what has become a multi-award-winning series.

Thank you, Charles Griemsman, my ever-patient editor. You get me, and I'm grateful for your insight, guidance and partnership.

Thank you, Stacy Boyd, for the opportunity to join this amazing stable of romance authors who feel like a family. And thank you for your diligence in making Harlequin Desire one of the most diverse romance imprints on the market today.

Thank you, Errin Toma, for your kindness, patience and quick responses whenever I need a question answered.

Thank you to Bill Laughton, Tony Horvath and the incredible Harlequin Desire art team for taking my vision for these characters and translating it so brilliantly into gorgeous, attention-grabbing covers that have helped readers discover the stories contained within.

One

Cole Abbott stepped down out of his crew cab truck, which towered over the other vehicles in the small parking lot of the Magnolia Lake General Store, and went inside.

He scrolled through a text message from his mother, Iris. Then he got a shopping cart and made his way through the store, picking up last-minute items for his family's weekly Sunday dinner.

Cole grabbed a few tubs of Häagen-Dazs vanilla ice cream, then went to find whipped topping. He dumped two cans into his cart, thought about it, then added another.

"I don't even want to know what you plan to do with those."

Cole turned toward the warm voice coming from

behind him. A voice that had always managed to be both teasing and reprimanding in a way that left him unsure of whether he was being teased or reprimanded. He blinked, barely able to believe his eyes.

"Renee? What are you…? I mean…*wow.* You look… amazing. Good to see you," Cole stammered. They shared an awkward hug that she leaned into, but extricated herself from just as quickly.

Renee Lockwood was both a ghost from his past and an enchanting vision in the present. He'd always liked Renee. A lot. But he hadn't ever dated her. She'd been his high school math tutor, a fellow member of his graduating class and the granddaughter of his mentor. They'd become friends. But he hadn't been a very good friend to her in the end. Something that often haunted him.

"Thank you." Renee spared him a faint half smile and raked her fingers through her glossy, dark hair, settling the strands over one shoulder. "Good to see you again, too."

Cole honestly might've walked right past Renee, not recognizing that she was the awkward, shy, geeky girl he'd once adored. In fact, not much about the woman standing before him resembled his old friend and tutor.

The Coke-bottle glasses and braces were gone. And Renee's boyish figure had been replaced by full breasts and curvy hips, her dark brown skin smooth and clear. Her inherent shyness seemed to be a thing of the past. Instead, she held her head high and her shoulders back. But her eyes still didn't quite meet his. Those almond-shaped eyes, shielded behind dark, thick lashes, had always fascinated him.

In school, to fit in she'd downplayed her excitement over math and science. But at her grandparents' kitchen table, she'd beamed as she waxed poetic about hypotenuse, integers and the periodic table. That year he'd even purchased a T-shirt for her birthday that bore the periodic table and the words, "I wear this shirt periodically. But only when I'm in my element." Ren had loved it, and Cole had loved seeing the way her eyes lit up whenever she wore it.

That shirt had kicked off his own obsession with smart-ass T-shirts, like the one he was wearing now beneath his button-down shirt.

"Family dinner," Cole finally blurted, in response to Ren's initial comment about the whipped cream. Though, now that he'd encountered her, he had some very different ideas about how to use it. When Renee raised an eyebrow in disbelief, Cole held up his phone, showing her the list. "My mother asked me to buy it."

"Hmm..." One side of Renee's mouth lifted in a reluctant smile. The kind he'd frequently teased out of her when she was trying to be serious and keep them on track so he'd graduate from high school on time, despite his academic struggles. "Ms. Iris asked for *two* cans of whipped cream." She held up two fingers. "That leaves one can unaccounted for."

Shit. She was right. He'd planned to take that last can home for... Well...you never knew when you might find yourself in need of a pressurized can of lickable sweets.

How the hell was Renee able to walk in here after

more than sixteen years and still read him like one of the algebraic equations she'd been able to solve without breaking a sweat?

"Relax, Cole. I'm kidding." Renee smiled, then leaned in and whispered, "No, I'm not."

It had been a running joke between them. Something he would often say because he couldn't help flirting with her, though he knew he shouldn't. They both laughed, and a little of the uneasiness between them seemed to dissipate.

"I saw your grandad the other day," Cole said, once the laughter between them had faded. "He didn't mention you were in town."

Renee lowered her gaze. "It was an unplanned visit. I arrived yesterday."

The Renee Lockwood he'd known hadn't done *anything* unplanned. She'd planned her life, her career and her day with precision.

Cole's gaze went immediately to her left hand and bare ring finger. "Sorry to hear about you and…"

"Dennis," Ren said the name as if it left a bitter taste in her mouth. "It's been over for a while. We made it formal a year ago. It was the best thing for everyone."

"Right." Cole hadn't met the man. But from what Ren's grandfather Milo had told him, Renee's ex was a golden boy. The only male heir of a wealthy family who'd made their money in pharmaceuticals. He hadn't much liked the man when his granddaughter had married him. Now Milo hated him.

Cole wanted to ask about her kid. Because it seemed

like the polite thing to do. But before he could ask, Renee changed the subject.

"Your family still does Sunday dinners, huh?" Ren smiled faintly. The sadness in her dark eyes made his chest ache. "It's sweet you all still get together for dinner once a week. Are all of your brothers and your sister still here in Magnolia Lake?"

"Yes. Blake is married with two kids. Parker is engaged to Kayleigh Jemison."

"I thought they hated each other."

"So did they." Cole chuckled.

"What about Max and Zora?"

"Max is seriously involved with Quinn Bazemore," Cole said.

Cole and Quinn had been close friends. He'd thought they might eventually end up together. But he hadn't known that his brother and Quinn had been involved the summer Max had been an intern at her grandfather's orchard. It had taken thirteen years, but Max and Quinn reconnected when their families collaborated to add fruit brandies to the King's Finest product line. Cole hadn't been thrilled when Quinn and Max started dating again. But the two were madly in love. He was happy for them.

"Quinn Bazemore…as in Bazemore Orchards?" Renee asked.

"Dixon's granddaughter," he confirmed. "And as for my baby sis…she and her best friend, Dallas Hamilton, got married in Vegas a few months ago. This is our first dinner since they got back from a four-month stint in Iceland for his work."

"That's wonderful." Renee's smile was reserved. Like she was happy for his siblings but maybe sad about the end of her own marriage. "And let me guess. You're the Abbott family's eternal bachelor."

Much to the chagrin of his mother and sister, *eternal bachelor* was a title Cole wore proudly. But something about hearing Ren say it made him uneasy.

"Clearly." He winked. "Gotta spread the love."

Renee rolled her eyes. "How selfless of you."

"You know me." Cole shrugged.

"I do." Ren studied him, her head tilted.

Translation: *I haven't forgotten what a jackass you were to me back then.*

Cole swallowed hard, his mouth falling open. He wanted to tell Renee he was sorry. To explain himself. But the words wouldn't come. He snapped his mouth shut, and she smirked. Probably because he was standing in the middle of the general store looking like a damn guppy.

"You must be eager to see Zora and her husband. I won't keep you." Ren shifted her purse to the other shoulder. "Guess I'll see you around." She turned and walked away.

Cole stopped himself from inviting Ren to dinner with his family. Because as much as he'd like to see more of Renee, he didn't want to give her or his family the wrong impression.

He liked Renee. Missed having her as a friend. Regretted that their friendship had ended the way it did. But he wasn't looking to get seriously involved with anyone. Least of all someone with wealthy, asshole ex drama and a kid.

No, sir.

Maybe the rest of his siblings had fallen victim to the love bug. But Cole was perfectly content with his life just as it was. Renee Lockwood's return wouldn't change that.

Cole bit his lip and sighed. He hated to see her leave, but as he watched the sway of Ren's full hips in her sexy little skirt, he definitely enjoyed watching her go.

Two

Renee stood in line at the general store, waiting to check out. But she couldn't help staring out the window at Cole loading his oversize pickup truck with its fancy wheels.

Boys and their toys.

Her ex had a stable of expensive classic cars he'd restored. He'd kept his favorites in the six-car garage of their home, built on his family's secluded estate. A light blue 1964 Aston Martin discovered in an old, rundown barn in Spain; a red 1968 Chevy Camaro; and a gorgeous blue 1965 Ford Mustang Shelby Cobra. All of which he adored far more than he'd ever really cared for her or their son.

Dennis's obsession with cars was his way of overcompensating for the fact that he was a real-life Tin

Man with no heart or soul, who was less than adequate in bed. What was Cole overcompensating for with his oversize truck? It didn't matter, because Cole Abbott was no concern of hers.

"Ma'am?"

The cashier's soft plea, accompanied by a big, friendly smile and a deep Central Tennessee twang, roused her from her thoughts. Renee's cheeks burned beneath the stare of the teenage cashier and the other shoppers in line.

"Sorry." Renee returned the girl's smile and set her basket on the counter so the cashier could ring her up. There was a tug on her skirt. Her little boy, Mercer.

"What is it, sweetheart?" She studied his handsome face, which bore features of both her and her ex. Yet, somehow, the boy was the spitting image of her grandfather. Something which had annoyed her ex to no end.

Four-year-old Mercer pointed out the window at the large black truck Cole was climbing into. "Vroom!"

Ren lifted her son, whose long legs dangled to her knees, so he could get a better view of the truck before Cole pulled off. "Truck," she said. "The big truck goes *vroom*."

The boy nodded, leaning his head against hers.

Ren kissed his temple before setting him back on the ground.

"Sorry, Renee. He got away from me. Took off the moment he saw you." Her grandmother hurried toward them, out of breath.

"It's okay, Gran. I should've warned you that Mercer is a little speed demon. Once he gets loose, he's off to the races."

The little boy looked up at his great-grandmother with an apologetic smile. He reached a hand out to her as a peace offering.

Renee tried to hold back a smile as she passed him over to her grandmother so she could pay for her groceries.

Her four-year-old son was autistic and mostly nonverbal. But he was a charmer who'd learned to communicate his desires clearly without saying a word.

"That's Cole Abbott's truck." Her grandmother nodded toward the truck pulling out of the lot.

"I know." Renee thanked the cashier and gathered her bags. "I saw him in the store earlier. He was picking up a few things for dinner with his family."

"How nice," Gran said, following her out of the store as they headed toward Ren's Midnight Silver Tesla 3. "We really should invite Cole over to—"

"*No*, Gran." Ren turned to her grandmother.

"No?" Her grandmother frowned.

"It's your house, so of course you can invite over whomever you want. But *please* don't try to set me up with Cole or anyone else. That's not why I'm here. Mercer is my focus. Everything I do in my life…it's only about what's best for him."

"The boy needs a father," Gran argued as they continued their trek toward the car.

"He *has* a father," Ren noted. "He just happens to be a shitty one," she added under her breath so neither her grandmother nor Mercer could hear.

Ren put the groceries on the back seat, then strapped Mercer in.

"I meant a *real* father." Her grandmother lowered her voice as they both slipped into their seats. "And you deserve a *real* husband. A man who is going to cherish you. Take care of you. Be a partner to you in raising your son."

Ren's chest ached as she considered all the ways her ex had been lacking in that regard. To say she'd chosen her mate poorly would be the understatement of the century. But she'd had an entire year to contemplate her failings. She'd come here, to the little town where she'd spent her teenage years, to escape her mistakes. She had zero interest in revisiting them with her grandmother now.

"I know you love us, Gran, and I appreciate that you want what's best for Mercer and me." Ren put a gentle hand on her grandmother's forearm. "But the last thing I need is the distraction of a relationship, especially with someone like Cole Abbott, who probably doesn't do relationships anyway."

"Yet." Gran held up a finger. "But when the right woman comes along, his skirt-chasing days will be over. You'll see." She chuckled. "So if you have any interest in—"

"I don't," Ren said quickly.

"But you did," her grandmother countered.

"I also once thought I could pull off a bra top and baggy jeans look, like Aaliyah. I was wrong about that, too."

"You wore what, now?" Her grandmother frowned.

"The point is...my crush on Cole was a lifetime ago, Gran. We're both different people now." Renee settled back against the black, vegan leather seat. "Scratch that... *I'm* a different person. I have serious responsibilities and ambitious goals. He's pretty much who he's always been. Playing the role of the carefree bad boy and loving it."

"That isn't fair, sweetheart." Gran buckled her seat belt. "I know the boy had his faults, but he's a good and kind man. Always has been. And he's got quite a bit of ambition of his own. He could've just taken some cushy job at his family's distillery. Instead, he built his own construction and development company."

"Because he bought Gramps's construction company and because Grandpa mentored him." Renee put on her seat belt and started the car.

"Cole's company had outgrown your grandfather's long before he purchased it. He didn't need your grandfather's business or his run-down equipment. Cole offered to buy the business as a courtesy to your grandfather. He even insisted on paying more than the business was worth. He wanted to ensure that we lived a comfortable life in retirement. And he's been there whenever we've needed him."

Her grandmother's mention of Cole being there was a silent reminder that she hadn't been. During her seven years of marriage to Dennis, she'd been notably absent from the lives of her own family.

Dennis hadn't liked coming to Tennessee to visit. Nor had he and his family been particularly delighted when her family had come to visit them. And if she was being honest with herself, she'd refrained from visiting her parents and grandparents alone because she hadn't wanted them to see the truth. That she was miserable because marrying into the Chandler family had been the biggest mistake of her life.

"Gran, I'm sorry I haven't been around more. But I'm here now and—"

"No need to apologize, sweetheart. I realize how difficult it must've been for you. I'm sorry your marriage didn't work out—I really am. But I'm glad to have you back here, where you and Mercer belong."

Renee blinked back tears. She glanced back at her son, who happily sucked his thumb. The corners of his mouth lifted in a little smile and he pointed forward.

Her son had a language all his own, and the gesture was Mercer for *Mommy, let's go already.*

"Gotcha, big guy." She checked the rearview mirror. "We're headed home to Grandpa."

Mercer's smile deepened and he kicked his feet happily.

Renee headed back to her grandparents' home, where she would make them a big, fancy gourmet meal, put Mercer to bed for the night, then try to convince her grandparents to let her revive their family farm.

Ren had spent her entire career as a pharmaceutical scientist researching and developing therapeutics for Alzheimer's disease while in pursuit of a cure. She'd made substantial contributions, of which she was proud. But with her son's autism diagnosis at the age of two, her focus had shifted. Her primary concern was Mercer and his future.

She had big plans for the property where generations of the Lockwood family had raised cattle and grown corn and soybeans. Resuscitating the farm would be a huge task. Especially since she'd be managing the project alone with the help of a few hired hands.

Between raising Mercer and managing the farm, there'd be no time for romance. So she'd dismiss her less-than-pure thoughts about how good Cole's rather impressive ass looked in those jeans. And how his button-down shirt had been just tight enough to accentuate his strong biceps and broad chest. She'd forget how handsome he'd looked with his trim beard and cinnamon-brown skin. But she'd remind herself of just how dangerous that devilish smile could be.

She was here to start a new life for herself and her son. Not to revisit old wounds or set herself up for new ones. That meant putting Cole in her rearview mirror and not looking back.

Three

"Hey, baby sis." Cole grinned as he opened his arms to his younger sister.

"Cole!" Zora leaped into his arms and gave him a bear hug. "I missed you, knucklehead." She grinned. "I worry about you when I'm not around. We both know you need constant supervision."

Cole chuckled. She wasn't wrong.

His younger sister was more of a hawk over him and his brothers than their parents were. Sometimes, he swore Zora thought *she* was their mother.

"What about those three?" Cole indicated his three brothers as they entered the den. Blake sat in a wing-back chair with his infant daughter, Remi, on his lap and his son, Davis, on the floor nearby playing with his toy cars and trucks. Max and Parker were seated on the sofa having a debate about something related to the distillery. Their grandfather occupied the other wingback chair. And their father, Duke, stretched out in his favorite recliner. “Why aren’t you worried about them?”

Zora propped a hand on her hip and cocked her head with a dramatic eyebrow raise. A silent *What do you think?*

Cole and Zora burst into laughter. Their older brothers were already low-key. But now that they were in committed relationships, they were total bores.

“Point made,” Cole said.

“Okay, what does today’s T-shirt say?” Zora asked impatiently.

Cole unbuttoned his shirt enough to permit his sister to see the words imprinted on the T-shirt he wore beneath it.

If you met my family, you’d understand.

Zora burst out laughing. She waved a hand. “No, sir. You will *not* blame your nonsense on us.”

“Hey, babe. Your mom needs you in the kitchen.” Dallas entered the room and slipped his arms around Zora’s waist from behind. He kissed her neck. “What’s up, Cole?”

Dallas extended a closed fist to Cole and he bumped it. Things were good between them again. But Cole and his brothers had initially been angry when their sister had returned home from spending her birthday weekend in Vegas suddenly married to her longtime best friend.

“Nuthin’ much.” Cole shrugged. “Also, I know she’s your wife, but that happens to be my baby sister. So maybe a little less of the PDA.”

“Hush!” Zora giggled as Dallas nuzzled her neck.

“Don’t be a jealous hater, bruh,” Max said on his way out of the room.

“I am not—”

Max was already gone before Cole could argue.

“Don’t worry, Cole. Your day is coming. Promise.” Zora’s warm smile radiated love and maybe a tiny bit of pity. “I’m gonna go see what Mama wants.”

Cole didn’t bother to respond. Growing the town one little person at a time had apparently become the mission of his siblings. He’d leave that to them. He was expanding the town in his own way. One home, one building, one community at a time.

And if things went his way, he’d leave behind an even greater legacy in the town of Magnolia Lake.

Cole helped his mother and Kayleigh clear the dishes from the table while Quinn and Blake’s wife, Savannah, brought out two pans of peach cobbler, dessert plates, the tubs of ice cream and the whipped topping.

“Everything okay, son?” his mother asked as she rinsed the dishes, then handed them to him so he could put them in the dishwasher.

“Everything is good.” Why were the women in his life so good at getting into his head?

“But there is *something* on your mind,” she pressed.

“I ran into Renee Lockwood at the general store.” He put another dish in the rack.

“I didn’t know Ren was back in town,” Iris said. “What a sweet girl. I was sorry to hear things didn’t work out with her husband. But I’m glad she’s come to spend some time with Milo and Janice. They could use the company." She turned off the water and looked over at him. "That must be the first time you've seen Renee in seventeen or eighteen years." She cocked her head. "You all right?"

"Why wouldn't I be?" Cole reached for another plate.

"You were quite fond of her in high school. I thought seeing her again might've brought up some…feelings for you."

"We were friends. That's all," Cole reminded her, his tone sharper than he'd intended. "After all, you thought I was wrong for her," Cole said bitterly. "And you were probably right."

"I *never* said that." His mother's voice was tight. "I said you shouldn't play with her emotions. Renee was obviously head over heels for you. But she was so bright and—"

"I wasn't." It pained Cole to say the words.

All the memories of his school struggles and the fights it had caused with his parents hit him squarely in the chest. Growing up, he'd been the Abbott family disappointment. He was the youngest boy and clearly hadn't lived up to the expectations his academically gifted brothers had established.

He didn't resent that his siblings were scholastic stars. But he'd been bitter no one seemed to understand that his underperformance wasn't because he was a slacker. He'd honestly been doing his best. But his family and teachers had all felt that if his brothers had excelled, why couldn't he?

Eventually, he'd leaned into the role of slacker. Because it was easier to pretend he didn't care than to admit he was struggling and needed help. He'd only accepted tutoring from Renee because Milo had insisted that he'd be helping her as much as she'd be helping him. Being a tutor looked good on her academic résumé.

"We pushed so hard because we knew how bright you were. We just wanted you to live up to your potential." His mother's eyes shone.

"You wanted me to live up to *your* expectations." Cole hated seeing the pain in his mother's eyes. But he'd tried hiding his feelings on the subject. It only led to resentment. Especially between him and his father. It'd taken years for their relationship to recover. He wouldn't go there again.

"You're right, sweetheart," she said. "You were meant for a different path, and we're proud of everything you've achieved." Iris handed him another dish. "And for the record, I *never* thought you weren't good enough for Renee, Cole. But you were both so young, and she was a brilliant young woman at an important crossroads in her life. I didn't want to see her get sidetracked."

The entire town had pinned their hopes and dreams on Renee, who was Ivy League bound. Just as they'd cheered on every other native who'd gone on to do great things. That kind of support and camaraderie was why, though he traveled the world and owned rental property in South Carolina, he would always call Magnolia Lake home.

"Did Renee say how long she's staying?"

"Didn't ask." Cole put the last of the dishes into the dishwasher and shut the door. But he'd wanted to.

"Just remember, son, Renee has been through a rough divorce, and she's raising a child on her own. She's not your usual conquest."

Before he could object to having a conversation about his sex life with his mother, Zora called them.

"Will you two hurry up? We're waiting for you."

"Would've gone faster if your impatient tail had helped us," his mother responded.

That shut his sister up.

His mother slipped her arm through his. "I was by no means a perfect mother, but I tried very hard to be the best mother I could be."

"And I'm lucky to have you and Dad as parents. I know you've made a lot of sacrifices to ensure that we had a better life." Cole kissed his mother's temple. "I'm glad you're finally fulfilling one of your dreams."

"Seeing all my babies happily married?"

"Real subtle hint, Ma." Cole chuckled. "I meant opening a restaurant like you've always wanted."

"Opening a restaurant in the same building where my dad once ran our little family café… It still feels like a dream. And to have your company renovating the space… It just doesn't get any better." She sighed happily.

Cole couldn't help grinning as they returned to their seats at the table, where everyone was waiting.

"We have *huge* news." Zora gripped her husband's hand and leaned into him. "We're pregnant."

"Oh my God, Zora!" Iris was on her feet in an instant, wrapping her daughter and son-in-law in a tight hug. Dallas's mother, Tish, hugged them next.

The family made the rounds congratulating the two as Zora informed them that her baby was due in about six months.

"I swear we aren't trying to steal your thunder here, Brat," Max said. "But Quinn and I have news of our own." He glanced over at Quinn with a dreamy look in his eyes. "I proposed last night, and Quinn accepted. We're engaged."

Quinn held up her hand and wiggled her fingers, displaying the ring. Evidently she'd just slipped it on, or Cole's mother and sister would've noticed it sooner.

"You two are getting married?" Zora practically squealed. "I'm so excited for you."

"Have you set a date?" Grandpa Joe asked as everyone gathered around to look at Quinn's ring.

"We'd like to get married around the anniversary of when we first reconnected," Quinn said.

"But that's in a few months," his mother noted. "The barn is booked every Saturday for the rest of the year."

"I know." Quinn slipped a hand into Max's. "And I realize how much the barn means to you. That it's where everyone else in the family has been married. But Max and I plan to get married at my grandfather's orchard, where this all began for us."

Quinn seemed to hold her breath as she awaited Iris's response.

"How romantic." Iris's eyes were wet with tears. "Let us know how we can help."

Quinn nodded, seemingly relieved.

"You're going to need a new plus-one," Zora said, so only he could hear her. Quinn had been his plus-one for both his cousin Benji's wedding and his parents' fortieth anniversary. "And Dallas's cousin Vanessa has been asking about you since she met you at our wedding here."

"I'm good, Zo. Thanks," Cole said.

Maybe now that Zora had her own bun in the oven, she could play mama bear to her own little cub and stop worrying over him all the time.

Cole ate his peach cobbler, piled high with whipped topping, in silence as his family chatted about another upcoming wedding and the impending arrival of Zora's baby.

It was official. With Parker and Kayleigh and Max and Quinn getting married in a few months, and Blake and Zora already married, he was the last lone wolf in the family.

Fine by him. He was content to be the best damn uncle that ever lived.

Four

"Dinner was delicious, sweetheart." Renee's grandmother stood to gather the dishes.

"Thank you, but you just relax, Gran." Ren stood. "I'll clear the table."

"I'd rather you have a seat and tell us what's on your mind." Her grandfather steepled his hands over his belly.

"How'd you—"

"When you were a teenager, you'd clean the house inside and out whenever you wanted to ask for something and you thought I was gonna tell you no." He chuckled. "I'll let you in on a little secret. Most of the time, I would've said yes anyway. Even without all of them extra chores."

Ren sank onto one of the wooden chairs her grandparents had owned for as long as she could remember. "I thought I'd wait until after I gave Mercer a bath and put him to bed."

They all looked at the little boy, who plucked a blueberry from the bowl in front of him and carefully examined it before popping it into his mouth. Mercer was a picky eater, but blueberries were his favorite.

"Is it something he shouldn't hear?" her grandmother asked. "Like something about his father?" She whispered the last word.

"This isn't about Dennis."

"Then no time like the present," her grandfather said.

All right. Here goes.

"I wanted to talk to you about the farm." She met her grandfather's stern gaze.

"What about it?" He sat up, giving her his full attention.

"I'd like to buy it."

Her grandparents exchanged a look of concern, then looked back at her.

"You'd like to buy the farm?" He repeated her words. "What on earth do you plan to do with it?"

"Restore it to a working farm again," she said matter-of-factly. "Only better."

"Better *how*?" Gran asked.

"I'll employ science and technology to make it a sustainable organic farm. One that will provide employment for neurodiverse men and women." She nodded toward her son.

Her grandparents' frowns eased and their eyes flickered with understanding.

"An admirable ambition, sweetheart." Milo's voice had softened. "And I can certainly understand why it would be so important to you." He glanced at Mercer, who contentedly picked through his blueberries without a care in the world. "But I don't think you realize what a monumental task it is to run a farm."

"Alone," Gran added. "We did it together for years, honey. It's an awful lot of backbreaking work."

"I know it won't be easy," Ren said. "But recent scientific breakthroughs and the latest technology will expedite things. And I'd hire knowledgeable, experienced help."

"Renee, sweetheart..." Gran was saying.

"Your grandmother says you ran into Cole earlier today. Did you two discuss the farm?" Milo rubbed his chin.

"Why would I discuss this with Cole?"

"Because he's been badgering me about buying that plot of land for the past two years." He folded his arms.

"Cole wants to buy *our* family farm? Why? Don't the Abbotts have enough land of their own?"

"He wants to turn it into a new community of luxury homes. Keeps going up on the offer every few months," he said.

"Do you plan to sell to him?" Ren asked.

"It's a tempting offer. But it don't sit quite right, selling the land that's been in our family for generations." Milo dragged a hand over his head. His gaze settled on her. "Don't seem right saddling you with it, neither. I know you're brilliant and determined, Renee. But it's a lot of work for a single—"

"Woman?" She narrowed her gaze at her grandfather.

"A single *parent*," he finished. "It's a much bigger undertaking than you seem to realize."

"I know it won't be easy, but I have a plan. I won't try to take on the entire thing at once. I would start with one of the smaller tracts of land your sisters lived on," Ren said.

Her great-aunts had owned two tracts of land sitting side by side, their homes fairly close. One great-aunt grew strawberries and blueberries, which local folks would often stop and pick for themselves. The other grew flowers, supplying florists in the region. They had a little stand out front where they'd often sit and chat while they waited for customers to stop by.

Her great-aunts, Wilhelmina and Beatrice, had been the last of her grandfather's siblings. They'd been gone for five years now, dying within months of each other. Her grandfather was now the sole owner of the entire parcel of connected farmland. He'd given up farming for construction many years ago and moved off his tract, so the land was in disuse and overgrown.

Milo's eyes were glossy at the mention of his sisters. "Hard to believe I'm the last man standing. All my brothers and sisters are long gone."

"I miss them, too. And I'd like to continue their legacy by growing fruits and vegetables like Aunt Willie and flowers like Aunt Bea."

"What you want to do is a nice tribute to your great-aunts and a wonderful thing to do for Mercer and other children and adults on the spectrum." Gran gripped her husband's free hand, recognizing he was too choked up to speak. “But honey, you already have your hands full with Mercer. How do you expect to—”

“I appreciate your concern, Gran and Gramps. But it’s no different than if I had a demanding full-time job. Which I did when Mercer was a baby. This way, even if I hire a nanny, I’ll just be steps away if Mercer needs me.”

Her grandfather sighed. “This plan you say you’ve got. Give me the quick and dirty version.”

Renee folded her hands on the table in front of her. “I’d start with growing organic carrots, tomatoes, cucumbers and berries along with companion flowers like marigolds and lilacs and herbs like basil and thyme. The companion plants will safely deter garden pests and can also be sold locally.”

“Any animals?” He rubbed his grizzled chin.

“I’d probably get a few chickens. For organic eggs, not for food,” she clarified.

“Free-range, I’d imagine.” The term was clearly suspect to Milo Lockwood.

“Supervised free-range, but yes. That’s the plan,” she confirmed.

“Nothing like how my parents did things or their parents before them. Why does everyone always want to change things?” he grumbled.

“So we don’t have to wash our clothes on a rock in a stream and dial rotary telephones on a short cord attached to the wall,” Ren teased.

“Now that’s *definitely* the kind of smartass answer I’d get from Cole.” The old man chuckled, as did her grandmother. Mercer, not wanting to be left out of the fun, laughed, too.

Renee ruffled her son's tight curls. "So what do you think, Grandpa?"

"You've given me a lot to consider. But I'll need some time to think on it, all right?"

Ren tried not to sound as defeated as she felt. "Yes, sir. Of course. I realize I sprung this on you seemingly out of nowhere. But I've been thinking about this for at least a year."

"Since the divorce." Her grandfather nodded. "Well, I promise to give your proposal fair consideration." He patted her hand, then stood and rubbed his rotund belly. "Gonna walk off some of that fine meal you made. Why don't I take Mercer?"

"He'd like that."

Her grandfather lifted Mercer from his booster seat and took his hand. "Coming, Janice?"

Gran looked to her. "You're sure you don't mind cleaning up by yourself?"

"Not at all. Enjoy your walk."

She grabbed a jacket for Mercer, who bounced up and down on his toes, excited about going for a walk. Then she slipped his little Skip Hop backpack over his arms and strapped the belt that spanned his chest before handing the attached tether to her grandfather.

"He's fast," she explained, when her grandfather looked puzzled. "That's so he doesn't get away from you."

"I don't need—"

"Trust me, we do." Gran took his free hand. "Now come on. It'll be dark soon."

"Have fun," Ren called after them. "Don't get into any trouble."

"Not making no promises." Her grandfather winked, slipping on his own jacket.

Renee gathered the dishes and took them to the kitchen. She rinsed them and loaded the dishwasher.

Why did her grandparents keep bringing up Cole Abbott? And there were countless plots of land in this county that Cole could build on. Why was he set on buying her family's land?

It didn't matter, because she was back in Magnolia Lake to stay, ready to put down roots. Her family was here. Though her dad and older brother, both still serving in the army, were stationed overseas, she had her grandparents, and her mother was just an hour away in Knoxville.

People in town had been nothing but kind to her and Mercer. They'd shown her son more consideration than his own father or paternal grandparents had. Mercer seemed happier and more relaxed, and so was she. The knot in her gut had loosened. Her shoulders and back didn't feel so tight. And she stood a little taller than when she'd first arrived, feeling worn-out and broken.

Here, in Magnolia Lake, was *exactly* where she and Mercer needed to be. Whether it took two days, two months or two years, she was determined to turn her dream of revitalizing the family farm into a reality.

Cole Abbott could go and turn someone else's family legacy into luxury villas.

Five

Cole made his way inside the Magnolia Lake Bakery and waved to the owner, Amina Lassiter.

"Your usual?" Amina asked.

"Please."

"I'll bring it to you, sugar. Grab a seat," Amina said before returning her attention to the customer she was waiting on.

Cole looked around and quickly spotted the man who'd summoned him here, the man to whom he owed his career, and in some ways, his life: Milo Lockwood. He was sitting in one of the booths near the back, but he wasn't alone.

He was with his granddaughter, Renee.

It'd been two weeks since they'd encountered each

other in the general store. Cole hadn't realized Ren was still in town.

He walked back to where they were seated and stood in front of their table.

"Good afternoon, Milo, Renee. If you need some time, I can grab something to eat first." Cole glanced at his watch. The Breitling Navitimer was a birthday gift from his brother Parker, who was obsessed with acquiring expensive watches from government auctions. "Or I can check on my crew's progress over at the restaurant and come back in an hour."

"No, son. You're right on time." Milo stood, gesturing to the other side of the booth where his granddaughter was seated. "Please, have a seat."

Renee gave her grandfather a pointed look and pressed her pouty lips into a hard line as she scooted over. She turned toward him.

"What brings you here this afternoon, Cole?"

"I was summoned." He nodded toward Milo.

"What a coincidence." Renee eyed the older man. "So was I."

Milo, who looked like he'd pulled a big joke on them, tried and failed to contain his grin.

"Well, now I'm really intrigued. He was pretty vague when he asked me to meet him here. I figured he just wanted to catch up," Cole said.

"And I assumed that this was about my proposal to buy the farm." Renee folded her arms on the table, still staring at her grandfather, who seemed endlessly amused.

Some things about Renee had changed. Being remarkably adorable, even when she was annoyed, apparently wasn't one of them.

"Wait...you offered to buy the Lockwood family farm holdings?" Cole's brain—distracted by Ren's enticing scent and how damn good the woman looked in her tortoiseshell cat-eye glasses—finally caught up. He turned toward her, and his knee brushed against hers beneath the table.

A jolt of electricity traveled up his thigh and settled into places it was best he didn't think about at the moment.

Renee reacted as if she'd felt it, too. She scooted toward the wall.

"Yes. It is *my* family's farm." She slapped an open palm to her chest. His gaze dropped to the hint of her full breasts revealed by a deep V-neck T-shirt.

He cleared his throat and forced himself to meet those mesmerizing, coffee-brown eyes.

"I've offered to buy the farm. Repeatedly," Cole informed her.

"I'm aware. Gramps told me two weeks ago when I made my offer." Renee sat taller in her seat and they both turned to her grandfather. "Which is why I'm surprised he invited us *both* here."

The old man shoveled the last spoonful of his baked-potato soup into his mouth, then took his time dabbing his lips with a napkin.

"I invited you both here because I've made a decision about how to handle you both wanting that land. I'm not a man who enjoys repeating himself unnecessarily," Milo said. "So I thought I'd tell you both at once."

"All right." Cole braced himself for the older man's decision. "Let's hear it."

"Both of your plans could be beneficial for Magnolia Lake. But I don't have enough evidence to determine which would be better."

Renee and Cole started speaking simultaneously, but Milo held up a hand, silencing them.

"I've come up with a plan to make a fair, well-informed decision," he said. "Just hear me out."

Shit. Cole definitely didn't like where this was going.

Milo had been a farmer for years, but he'd quit the farm and had been working in construction for well over a decade by the time Cole had begun working for him. The old man had generously taught Cole everything he knew about building and construction. He'd shown Cole how to be a good businessman and an upstanding individual through object lessons. Cole had a strong sense he was in store for yet another.

"Okay, Grandad." Renee leaned back against the booth and sighed. "We're listening."

A wide smile spread across the man's face and his gold tooth sparkled in the sunlight streaming from the window. He clapped his hands together, then leaned forward, studying each of their faces.

"There's an awful lot of land. I could divide the plot, giving you each half of it to develop your chosen project," Milo said.

So he was going King Solomon on them. Under different circumstances that might've been okay. But not for what Cole had in mind.

"That won't give me enough land for this project. I'm

building an entire community of luxury homes about the size of my parents' house," Cole said.

"That would certainly bring in a lot more revenue around here. Maybe help the town finally get that new bridge, so we won't have to worry about the old one washing out whenever the river floods." Milo nodded thoughtfully.

"My plans are just as beneficial for the town," Renee piped up. "The wealthy can take care of themselves, believe me," she added bitterly. "My plan is better for the environment and it's an opportunity to improve the lives of those who actually could use our assistance." Her eyes gleamed with what looked like tears.

Cole fought back the urge to squeeze her hand. For all he knew, Renee was playing them both. Though that didn't track with the girl he'd once known.

Still, this was a business deal, pure and simple. And he was prepared to pay Milo Lockwood handsomely for the prime location.

"If it's a matter of the price—"

"It isn't." Milo seemed insulted by the insinuation that money alone would sway his decision. "It's about what's best for the community."

Cole nodded. "Of course."

"I don't want to split the property, either," Renee concurred. "I'd start slowly with the organic farm. But I plan to use the entire plot. Besides, I doubt Cole's wealthy residents would want to live next door to my berry bushes and free-range chickens."

"You want to turn the land back into a working farm? *Alone?*" Cole eyed her.

"Yes, I plan to revive the family farm," Her tone was indignant and there was fire in her dark eyes. "And do you build your houses alone?"

"Fair," Cole said. "But managing a farm is a lot of work for a—"

"If you say a single mother, I swear to God…"

Milo chuckled. "My granddaughter is a bit sensitive about this. You don't want to challenge her on it, believe me. Janice and I learned that the hard way."

"Fine." Cole threw his hands up. "Farming is a lot of work. *Period.* Whether you're doing the work yourself or not. I'd hate to see you get in over your head with this, Renee."

"And I'd hate to see you turn my family's legacy into a bunch of in-ground pools and tennis courts for trust fund babies and socialites, *Cole.*" She folded her arms over her chest.

Cole returned his attention to Milo and tried not to think about how gorgeous Ren looked in the simple long-sleeve T-shirt and pair of jeans. Or how amazing she smelled. Or how much he'd like to hear her say his name, just like that, but in a very different setting.

Mind out of the gutter, man. Mind out of the gutter.

"It was a fair idea, Milo. But splitting the land doesn't seem to work for either of us." Cole stated the obvious.

"Thought you two might say that."

"So how can I convince you that reviving the family farm is the better option?" Renee asked her grandfather.

"Or that turning that land into high-end residential homes will significantly increase the per capita income of Magnolia Lake so we can improve the town's infrastructure?" Cole interjected.

"King's Finest Distillery is the largest employer in town. One would think that KFD would contribute to building up the infrastructure." Renee leaned back against the booth, her arms still folded.

Cole was the only member of his family who didn't work for their world-renowned distillery. However, it was a universally acknowledged rule that you got to talk shit about your family but other people didn't.

"They do. In addition to being the largest employer—which pays its workers quite generously, by the way—my family has done *a lot* for this town. Always has. Always will." He turned to her again, folding his arms, too.

"Many of the businesses in town have been recipients of grants, loans and business mentoring sponsored by King's Finest. My business included," Milo acknowledged. "That's how I was able to get started in construction when I was drowning in debt from the farm."

Renee's eyes widened. "I never knew that, Gramps."

"I never wanted you to." Milo sighed heavily. "Things were rough in those days. You were just a little girl then. I'd never have started my construction business without KFD's helping hand. That's why your grandfather felt betrayed when I gave you an option for building yourself a career outside of the distillery." He nodded toward Cole.

"I know." Cole sighed.

When he was a teenager, there was a point at which his grandfather and Milo had nearly come to blows.

Milo and Grandpa Joe's relationship was cordial now. But it had been hell being caught up in the animosity between two men he greatly admired.

"Here's what I plan to do." Milo reached into his jacket and pulled out a piece of paper. He unfolded it and pointed to one of two homes he'd sketched. "This here is Wilhelmina's old house. Right next door is Beatrice's old place. The rest of this sheet represents the remaining property.

"Renee, you say you'd like to continue the legacy of your great-aunts. Fine. Move into Willie's old place and prove that you can turn that overgrown jungle of hers into a viable organic farm."

Renee nodded thoughtfully. "I'd planned to start with a section about that size anyway. So that'd work for me."

"I can't very well take the other plot and build on it without knowing *exactly* what your plans are for the remaining land," Cole said.

He'd expected Renee to have the edge, but this was ridiculous. Why present it as a fair challenge when he didn't have a shot in hell of winning this thing?

"No, but you can renovate and restore that property any way you choose," Milo said.

"I'd end up tearing down the place if I wanted to build on the land later," Cole argued, annoyed that Renee was grinning, as if she'd already won.

"Those two houses *must* stand," Milo said, his voice filled with emotion. "My sisters would've wanted that. They loved that land. Devoted their entire lives to it. I can't let anyone tear down their homes. It's all I have left of them." Milo cleared his throat. "But whichever one of you impresses me most, that's who I'll sell the remaining property to."

Cole frowned. The old man had just gotten choked up about losing his sisters and being the last living member of his family. He could hardly pummel him with a barrage of questions or complain that this wasn't a fair fight.

Renee was swimming across the river in a tiny bathing suit and he was forced to wear a pair of lead shoes.

Bad choice of metaphor. Now he couldn't stop imagining Renee with all those delicious curves wearing a little bikini.

Cole squeezed his eyes shut and dragged his fingers back and forth across his forehead a few times as he considered his response.

"I was hoping to buy the entire block of properties, Milo. Including the plots these two houses occupy." Cole indicated the houses sketched on the sheet.

"I know, but I just can't bear to see those homes destroyed." He shrugged. "Still leaves plenty of land, though."

True.

"I think it's a brilliant idea, Gramps. Mercer and I can move into Aunt Willie's old place. Make it a home again."

"I'm banking on that." Her grandfather winked. "In fact, you would both need to live in your respective houses for six months, then I'll decide."

"What?" they asked simultaneously.

"I already have a place," Cole said.

"Which you've put up for sale." Milo grinned at him like the Cheshire cat. "You've been moving from one long-term flip to another for the past five or six years. Think of Bea's old place along the same lines. Keep the same footprint, add to it, whatever you want. Just... *don't* tear the old place down."

Cole's hands clenched into fists on his lap beneath the table. He wanted the land; he *really* did. He'd been practically stalking Milo for the past couple of years, hoping to acquire it.

He'd completed some breathtaking projects: his parents' home, his cousin Benji's multimillion dollar mansion, two new multiuse shopping centers that included both storefronts and condos. He had the restaurant renovation for his family, just across the street. However, with this project he hoped to leave his mark on the town and create a legacy of his own. The way his family had with King's Finest.

But maybe it just wasn't worth all this. After all, if he'd liked being told what to do and how he had to do it, he'd be working for his family at KFD. But his grandfather's and father's "my way or the highway" stance had prompted him to forge his own path. He had great respect for Milo, but bristled at the idea of being forced to play by the old man's rules. Particularly when Milo wasn't showing his hand.

"Grandad, Cole and I both think the world of you, and we appreciate your wisdom." Renee glanced at Cole. "But we aren't teenagers anymore. We're busy current and future business owners. So could we cut to the part where you explain the point of this little next-door neighbor experiment?"

Renee spoke calmly, but Cole could feel the tension rolling off her. She was as frustrated as he was.

"If the town of Magnolia Lake is going to continue to grow and thrive, we need plans like Cole's to make it happen. I love the prospect of a shiny new bridge that won't flood out and a fancy new shopping center. But I'm not willing to lose our precious way of life to make it happen." Milo huffed. "The sense of community and family we got in this town… Ain't no amount of growth and new infrastructure in the world worth sacrificing that."

The old man shifted his gaze between them. Both knew better than to interrupt during his long pause.

"I've seen what rapid growth can do to small towns like ours, and I don't want that. What we have here is worth fighting for. But we have to be smart about how we wage this battle." Milo tapped his temple with two fingers. "Gotta accept that change is inevitable, even necessary. But we must grab it by the reins and direct it carefully. That way, we keep what's best about this town and who we are while embracing the future."

"I agree with all of that, Gramps," Renee said. "But why does that require Cole and I to jump through these elaborate hoops?"

Milo shook his head, as if disappointed they didn't get it. "You two represent the future of this town. And if I can drill that lesson into the two of you…then maybe other folks will get it, too. We can expand the town while saving it from any negative impacts of that growth."

Cole pushed to his feet and checked his watch. He needed to do a walk-through over at the restaurant to make sure things were on track for the grand opening in the fall, then he needed to do a final inspection of Benji and Sloane's home since they'd be returning from Japan in just a few days. Not to mention the three other projects he was currently managing. He didn't have time for…whatever this was.

"Look, Milo, I appreciate how much you care about this town. I do, too. I would never do anything to hurt it or the people here. But what you're asking… It's a lot. I don't know if I'm prepared to…"

"Giving up already, Cole?" Milo asked with a chuckle. "Thought you were tougher than that. Afraid you'll have to go a few weeks without your fancy spa tub and *bidet*?"

Cole frowned, one eye twitching as Milo and Renee chuckled at his inference that Cole had somehow gone soft. That he was a pretty boy who couldn't rough it for a few weeks in the old house in dire need of renovations.

He was not amused.

"My resiliency isn't the issue here," Cole said. "You know how much I love and respect you. But like you always taught me…this is business and time is money. There has to be a more efficient way to resolve this issue."

"Nope." The stubborn old coot leaned back in the booth and folded his arms, like Cole's four-year-old nephew, Davis, when instructed to eat his brussels sprouts. "If you feel like my request is somehow beneath you...well, I guess you've proved my point. That maybe you aren't in touch with who we are and what we need in this town. Which makes me worry about that project you got planned."

Cole narrowed his gaze at Milo.

He had to admit, that shit hurt. Like his mentor had just plunged that fork on the table in his gut. Still, he wouldn't allow the old man to manipulate him.

"I'll think about it," Cole said.

"Give you a week to decide." A sly smile lifted one corner of Milo's mouth.

Cole slid on his shades and said his goodbyes to Milo and his granddaughter before grabbing his order to go. The one thing that gave him a perverse sense of satisfaction was the fact that Renee looked like she was fit to be tied.

Damn.

The visual of Renee tied up in his bed would definitely be stuck in his head.

Six

Cole stood in front of the abandoned home that had once belonged to Renee's great-aunt Ms. Bea. He vaguely remembered the older woman as being a little eccentric and always smelling like lavender.

He'd come here with his mother a few times. Beatrice grew the most beautiful flowers, which his mother had always adored. Right next door, her sister, Ms. Willie, grew some of the sweetest, most delicious berries he'd ever tasted.

The remnants of their little stand still stood out by the road on the property Milo had given his granddaughter.

Cole glanced over at Ms. Willie's place, less than a stone's throw from where he stood. The houses were surprisingly close together, given that each property was nearly two acres. He was torn about this idea of living so close to Ren for the next six months.

"You've changed your mind." Renee was standing in the yard of the house next door.

How had he not noticed her?

"Haven't decided." He shrugged. "But I promised your grandad I'd at least take a look at the place."

"So what's the verdict?"

"Too early to say." Cole shifted his gaze to the overgrown yard and then to the old farmhouse with its peeling paint and missing porch boards.

He'd expected to look at the place and immediately deem it worthy of a wrecking ball. But there was something about it he found intriguing. Or maybe it was the nostalgia of coming here as a kid.

"I'm surveying the property first. Then I'll take a look inside."

"I'd like to see the place, too, if you don't mind," she said.

"Afraid I got the better plot?" He raised a brow.

"She was my great-aunt, and I haven't seen the place since…" Her words trailed off.

"Of course." Cole cursed himself silently for being an insensitive jerk. "Take your time. I'll wait for you before I go inside."

Ren thanked him but she'd already walked toward her property before he could reply.

He'd told himself that he'd hoped to avoid Ren, but the truth was that a part of him was anxious to see her again. The part of him that missed the hours spent at her grandparents' kitchen table talking comic books and sci-fi shows and debating the superiority of the Marvel versus the DC universe. How she'd made learning fun for him by incorporating the things he enjoyed, like badass superheroes and sports, into their lessons.

But if starting something with Ren had been a bad idea then, it was a horrible idea now. Ren was still his mentor's granddaughter. Plus, she was a single mom divorced for a year. Not the kind of woman he normally hooked up with.

So he'd keep things casual and hope they could eventually reestablish the friendship that had once meant so much to him.

Cole walked around the building, assessing the property and its overgrown acreage. When he returned to the front of the house, Renee was seated on the front steps clutching her hands, one knee bouncing. Her worn jeans were smudged with dirt, as was her oversize navy T-shirt. She stood, her shoulders stiffening and her expression suddenly grim.

"Maybe we should do this some other time." Cole tilted the heavy planter on the front porch and retrieved the spare key Milo had left him. "And if you don't want me to go in without you, I'll put the key back and we can try this another day."

Her expression of distress morphed into one of shock. "You'd put off checking out the house just because…" Renee dropped her gaze from his for a moment. "No, I need to do this. But thank you."

"All right." Cole unlocked the front door and pushed it open.

The house was musty and stale, like every other old

house he'd acquired. Particles of dust floated on the air, disturbed by the gentle gust that blew in through the open door.

The place was neat and orderly, but it looked as if it'd been frozen in time.

Renee's soft gasp drew his attention. One hand covered her mouth, and her eyes were misty.

Of course, it was an emotional moment for her. Ren had always spoken so fondly of her eccentric great-aunts. Neither of them had children of their own, so Renee had been their grandchild by proxy. They'd doted on her and had been there to celebrate every single success in her life.

"It seems so surreal," she whispered, venturing deeper inside the house with small steps. Her lips curved into a small smile as she ran her hand over the old-fashioned rotary telephone on the hall table. "Still in perfect shape," she marveled, then laughed. "My parents bought them both cordless phones for Christmas one year. They're probably still in the boxes somewhere."

"I never got to tell you how sorry I was about your great-aunts," he said softly. "I saw you at the funeral with your husband. But—"

"We didn't stay long," she said abruptly, her eyes welling with fresh tears. "Dennis didn't do well outside of his own element. And *this*—" she held up her open palms "—definitely wasn't his element. We were back on his family's private plane not long after the service ended. So if you think I intentionally slighted you, you're wrong. I didn't."

That was exactly what he'd thought. But there was no need to say as much.

"I assume your family wants all the furniture. There are some valuable antique pieces here. Is Ms. Wilhelmina's house like this, too, with all of the furniture still in place?"

Renee lowered her gaze and shrugged. "I'm not sure. I haven't been able to bring myself to go inside." She seemed embarrassed by the admission. "I've been here three times in the past week. I walk the property and look at the old outhouses. Make my plan for what I'll plant and where. But the one thing I can't seem to do is—"

"Go inside." Now he understood why she'd been so eager to enter the house with him. "Look, I know you lost your aunts a long time ago, but in some ways, this must all still seem fresh to you."

She dabbed at her eyes with the back of her hand.

"It's like I'm just processing their loss. My grandparents offered to come to the house with me, but they already think I can't handle this. Admitting I couldn't even bring myself to go inside wouldn't inspire much confidence."

"I get it." Cole checked his watch, then glanced around. "I'll tell you what. We'll take a basic inventory of Bea's place. You tell me what your family would like to keep and what we can donate, sell or give away. Then we'll do the same thing over at Ms. Wilhelmina's."

"You realize that'll take hours," Ren said.

"I know." It wasn't how he'd intended to spend the rest of his afternoon. But he wasn't about to leave Ren out here wandering the property alone. "Why? Did you have to get back to your kids?"

"Kid," she corrected him. "I have one son. But I would assume you have some work project or maybe a hot date."

"I did."

"A business project or a hot date?"

"Both." He gave Ren a knowing smile. She was fishing. Trying to find out whether he was involved with someone. "Nothing that can't be rescheduled. Give me a minute to—"

"You don't need to do that, Cole. I'm being a baby about this. Now that I've been inside Aunt Bea's place, I know what to expect. It'll be fine."

"I know I don't have to. I want to. You helped me out of a tough jam. I wouldn't have graduated on time if it weren't for you. This is the least I can do."

"You realize your parents paid me to tutor you in math and science, right?"

"Of course." He chuckled. "But I'd like to think that we're friends, too." He shrugged. "What kind of friend would I be if I wasn't willing to help you out of a jam?"

"Thanks, Cole. That means a lot. But if I accept your offer, there's one thing you need to understand."

"Okay." He folded his arms, his feet planted wide as he prepared himself for the imminent *there is nothing happening between us* speech.

"This farm is just as important to me as this luxury development is to you. So don't think you can be all cute and charming and helpful or whatever and I'll fall on my fainting couch and concede."

"First, what the hell is a fainting couch?" He furrowed his brows as he considered the possibilities. "Second, you just called me cute *and* charming, so I'm pretty sure I'm winning."

"Oh my God. Seriously? *That's* what you got out of what I just said?" Renee propped a fist on one hip. She shook her head and sighed. "And *that's* a fainting couch." She pointed to what looked like a burgundy loveseat and her gaze softened. "It was Aunt Bea's favorite piece of furniture."

"So a chaise, then?"

"More of a daybed in the Victorian era," she said. "But totally beside the point. The point is, we're still on opposite sides of this thing, and only one of us can walk away the winner. I fully intend for that to be me. So maybe we call a little truce right now to help each other get settled into our places. But then it's game on."

"Fine." Cole tried to hold back his smirk. Renee was apparently just as competitive now as she had been back then. "But you said that we're helping each other out. What exactly is it that you plan to do for me?"

She turned her back to him as she glanced around the house. "Since you were willing to rearrange your schedule today to help me out… I'll help you sort through this stuff and clean up the place so you can move in. That is, if you've decided to move in."

Cole stared at Renee. He almost had the feeling she *wanted* him to say yes. Maybe he was making one hell of a mistake.

"Looks like I am, neighbor." Cole smiled. "I've got

a notebook and pen out in the truck. Why don't I grab it? Then we can start tagging everything."

Renee nodded, her sensual lips curving in a grateful smile.

And just like that, Cole knew he was already in way over his head.

Seven

Ren sat on the dated shag carpet covering the floor of her Aunt Willie's old bedroom with her legs folded. She carefully sorted through a box of photos she'd found in the closet.

"Those photos are fascinating. Are they all family members?"

Ren was startled by Cole's voice. He leaned against the door frame holding two paper cups.

How did the man manage to look so incredibly delicious in a pair of distressed jeans, a pair of old Timbs and a white T-shirt that read "I'm not lazy. I just entered energy-saving mode"?

Seriously, it was criminal. Or maybe her own personal sex drought had her hallucinating, like a parched woman wandering the desert.

Yes, Cole was hot. That was an indisputable fact. But he was also trouble. She was thirty-four years old and she'd never dated a single bad boy in her entire life. Her high school crush on Cole had been her first and last foray into the world of bad boys. It had reminded her that she wasn't the kind of girl that guys like Cole Abbott went for. They'd flirt a little to get her to help them with their homework, but there would be no dates to prom or homecoming weekends.

"Yes," Ren said finally, when Cole started to look worried by how long it had taken her to respond. She pushed up her glasses, which she'd worn because she'd forgotten to order a new supply of contacts. "Aunt Willie was apparently the Lockwood family historian. I'm going to take these to Gramps and see what he wants to do with them."

Cole ventured inside the room. He handed her one of the paper cups from Magnolia Lake Bakery, where he'd stopped to get them coffee each of the past three mornings they'd worked together to clear out Aunt Bea's place and the sheds on her farm. All of which would soon belong to Cole.

They were done at Aunt Bea's. The furniture had either been donated or stored in a shed on Ren's property; she'd decide whether to sell it or keep it later.

"Thank you." Ren accepted the cup, the scent of hazelnut rising with the steam as soon as she flipped open the lid. "But we're finished with your place. Didn't expect to see you this morning."

She blew into the cup of hot coffee, and she could swear that Cole's already dark eyes went darker.

He got down on the floor and sat beside her. Close enough that his clean, fresh scent tickled her nostrils, but not close enough that his legs touched hers. "You spent three days helping me clean up my place. You didn't think I'd just abandon you to do all this on your own, did you?"

"You're a busy CEO," she said.

"And you're a busy mom in the midst of starting her own company." He sipped his coffee.

Her heart fluttered a little in response to the acknowledgment. She felt seen in a way she hadn't in so long. Especially since she'd taken a leave at the lab to care for her son full-time soon after he was formally diagnosed as being on the autism spectrum.

Taking time off was a luxury most families didn't have. Dennis and his family hadn't appreciated her taking it. They'd urged her to let the nanny care for Mercer, so she could continue to head up their lab. But after her son had gotten burned and neither the nanny nor Dennis, who'd also been home at the time, knew how it had happened, she hadn't trusted anyone else to take care of her child.

It had even been hard for her to leave Mercer with her grandparents while she worked on getting Aunt Wilhelmina's house ready.

"I was surprised you did the cleaning and sorting yourself." She nodded toward the house just across the way. "Don't you have a crew to do that kind of thing?"

"On my commercial projects, yes. But this project is personal." He glanced over at her and her skin warmed.

"Why?" Ren couldn't help asking. "I know you have

to live here for six months. But you're only doing it to acquire the land, which makes it business."

"I didn't think you'd want a crew of burly guys trampling through your aunt's home and manhandling her things." Cole sipped more of his coffee.

There was that damn fluttering in her chest again. Because what an incredibly sweet thing for him to have done. He'd given up three days' worth of his valuable time and had rescheduled several work meetings and at least one date to make her more comfortable during this process. His thoughtfulness meant more to her than words could say.

"Thank you for taking my feelings into consideration, Cole. But you know I would never have expected you to do this."

"I know." There was something so warm and sweet in his dark gaze. Now there was a fluttering in her tummy, too. "But I wanted to. Or maybe I was just looking for an excuse to spend more time with you." He gave her shoulder a teasing nudge.

"Why?" Maybe it was a stupid question. But she needed to know why Cole Casanova Abbott would want to spend his Saturday morning navigating old photos and chasing dust bunnies with her. After all, he'd probably just tumbled out of the bed of some trust fund heiress and social media influencer who modeled in her spare time.

He smirked and for the first time in her life, Ren truly understood the term *devilishly handsome.*

"You're gonna make me say it, huh?" He chuckled softly. "Okay, here goes. I miss those afternoons hanging out with you. That's when I first learned to get comfortable with just being myself. Accepting every part of who I am."

"A rebel with a cause who loved the *Godfather* movies and gangsta rap but also geeked out on all things superhero and sci-fi." Ren smiled as she put the lid on the box of photos and set down her coffee. "I appreciate the credit, but I'm not sure I understand how I helped."

"By accepting me for who I was. By never looking down on me because I learned differently. By gassing me up whenever I was down on myself." Cole set down his cup and turned to her. "My mother taught us to always be kind to people because you never knew the impact even the smallest act of kindness could have on a person. Our short-lived friendship had a huge impact on me. On how I saw myself. On what I believed I could achieve."

She was incredibly moved by his words. "I had no idea."

"By the time I was able to pinpoint exactly why my life got better...you were already long gone. So I never got a chance to thank you for everything you did for me." Cole ran a hand through his mass of dark curls, which he'd always worn a bit longer on top than his brothers.

Ren's mouth was dry. Her heart thudded as her gaze was drawn to Cole's full lips.

Over the past few days, she'd been reminded of how desperately she'd wanted to know what it would be like to kiss Cole. This moment between them felt like the perfect time to find out.

Renee's eyes drifted shut as she pressed her mouth to his in a tentative kiss. She drew back, her eyes fluttering open when Cole didn't react. He stared at her, his chest quietly heaving.

Her face warmed and her stomach churned. Ren pressed another kiss to Cole's lush lips.

He leaned in closer and her glasses shifted, sitting askew on the bridge of her nose. His mouth curved in a half grin. He removed her glasses, then cradled her face in his hands as he kissed her again.

Cole was now clearly the one in control. With his fingers on the back of her neck and his thumbs against her cheekbones, he gently tilted her head. His lips, firm and lush, glided against hers.

It was all lips, no tongue. And yet her skin felt like it was on fire. Her nipples tightened and the space between her thighs grew damp.

Cole was an exceptionally good kisser. Even better than she had imagined all those nights she'd lain in her bed staring at the ceiling as a teenager. Regretting that she hadn't been brave enough to do just this.

Now that she had, she wanted more.

Ren parted her lips on a soft gasp and pressed a hand to Cole's chest. He sucked her lower lip between his, then gently sank his teeth into it, just shy of breaking the skin. He tightened his grip on the back of her neck and ran his tongue along the seam of her lips in a delicious, torturously slow movement that was driving her insane with want.

She parted her lips farther, making it clear she wanted him to deepen their kiss.

Suddenly, the wooden back screen door slammed, followed by her grandmother's distinct voice. "Renee, sweetheart, we're here. Mercer wanted to bring Mommy lunch."

Renee groaned quietly, pulling away.

She was thirty-four years old, and her grandparents still had an uncanny knack for ensuring she wouldn't get beyond first base.

Or maybe they had saved her from making a huge mistake. She was a single mom with responsibilities and a to-do list as long as her arm. She barely had the time and energy to deal with everything currently on her plate. She didn't have room in her life or time in her day for whatever she was doing now.

"Coming, Gran!" She called downstairs, then sighed softly as she turned back to Cole. She lowered her voice. "I'm sorry. I shouldn't have… I'm sorry," she said again.

Cole stood, then pulled Ren to her feet. "We were reminiscing about the past and got caught up in the moment." He shrugged.

"Right." She nodded. Maybe randomly kissing people was a regular thing for him. For her it was an anomaly. "We should probably head downstairs."

"You should probably go first. And take the photos. They'll be too distracted to worry about what we were doing up here." Cole handed her the box and her glasses.

Clearly, he'd done this before.

Ren made her way down the stairs with Cole lagging behind.

"Hi there, sweetheart." Her grandmother grinned broadly as she wiped down the kitchen table with a sponge. "Cole?" Her grandmother dropped the sponge in a bowl of hot, soapy water in the sink, then dried her hand on a dish towel. "Didn't realize you were here. In fact, Milo saw your truck and assumed you were next door. He took Mercer over to check on you."

"Mercer? Is that your little boy?" Cole asked.

"Yes." Ren's mouth curved in an involuntary smile whenever she thought of Mercer's wide eyes and contagious grin. "He's four."

"If you hurry, you can catch up with him," her grandmother said, lifting a picnic basket from the counter and setting it on the table. "Then you're welcome to come back here and join us for an early lunch. I brought plenty. Leftovers from last night. Smothered pork chops, loaded mashed potatoes and butter beans."

"Yes, ma'am." Cole grinned, leaning in to kiss the older woman on the cheek. "You know how much I love your cooking. You don't have to ask me twice."

Her grandmother giggled, then shooed Cole away. Evidently, she wasn't the only woman in the Lockwood family who'd been charmed by Cole Abbott.

"Are you blushing, Gran?" Renee grinned once the screen door slammed behind Cole.

"Don't try to change the subject." Her grandmother narrowed her gaze at her as she pulled items from the basket and laid them out on the table. "It took you two an awful long time to come down those stairs."

"Cole is helping me get the house ready. Since I helped him, he wanted to return the favor."

"But—"

"And look what I found." Renee held up the large

wooden photo keepsake box engraved with the words Lockwood Family.

"Oh my gosh." Gran placed a hand over her mouth. "Your grandfather and I bought that for Wilhelmina one Christmas, ages ago. I didn't realize she still had it."

"Well, she did. And look what she kept inside." Renee slid the engraved lid from the box, revealing the treasure trove of photos inside.

"I knew she'd been collecting family photos, but my goodness. Wait until your grandfather sees them."

"I know. I can't wait to show him." Renee beamed. "But in the meantime, I'll help you get lunch ready."

Renee washed her hands at the old farmhouse sink. She gazed at the two acres of farmland behind the house, wondering what her great-aunts would think of her plan to revive the farm.

It was better than reliving her ill-advised kiss with Cole. A mistake she knew she shouldn't repeat.

Eight

Cole stepped onto the back porch of Renee's house and dragged a hand across his lips.

That had been…*unexpected.* Since her return, Renee had been cold and distant. Not surprising, given how their friendship had ended. But over the past week, tension between them had eased and Ren had warmed up to him. Cole was grateful for that. Still, he hadn't expected Renee to kiss him. He sure as hell hadn't intended to kiss her back.

Since their encounter at the general store, Cole had been reminding himself of all the reasons Renee was off limits. Two of them stood a few yards away.

Cole jogged over to his Dodge Ram 1500 TRX Crew Cab 4x4, which sported twenty-inch rims with candy-apple-red accents. Milo was standing beside the truck, holding the little boy's hand. *Renee's* little boy. The kid had his mother's almond-shaped eyes and her heart-stopping smile. He bounced up and down excitedly on his toes as he pointed to Cole's truck.

"Vroom!" the little boy said.

"Hey there, Milo." Cole shook the older man's hand, then turned his attention to the child, whose gaze was still on the truck. "Hey there, little guy. You must be Mercer."

When he didn't respond, Cole turned back to Milo. "I'm not quite as interesting as the truck." Cole grinned. "I guess if I was four, I'd feel the same way."

"Don't take it personally, son." Milo chuckled. "Mercer here don't speak much. Nonverbal, they call it. But he does say a few things, like—"

"Vroom!" Mercer said again. Only this time, he wasn't pointing at the truck. He was pointing at Cole.

Cole smiled. "Hey there, Mercer. It's good to meet you. I'm Cole."

"Vroom!" Mercer said, then pointed to the truck.

"I think he's asking you to fire up that oversize machine of yours," Milo explained.

"Oh, so you're a car man." Cole nodded. "I can respect that. Would you like to climb inside with me?" Cole reached out a hand, but Mercer stepped back, wrapping an arm around his great-grandfather's leg.

The boy peeked at Cole, just one eye visible from behind the old man's leg. Mercer pointed at the truck again and repeated his request.

"You've got it, little man." Cole winked. The truck was a favorite of his nephew, Davis—his brother Blake's four-year-old son. Cole climbed into the truck and turned it on, the engine roaring.

The little boy giggled as he jumped up and down, bouncing on his toes as Milo held on to his hand.

Cole pulled the truck forward and back a few times there in the driveway before killing the engine and climbing out of the cab.

Mercer clapped and cheered.

"Gran sent me out here to collect the three of you for lunch," Renee said. "What's Mercer so excited about?"

"Cole here gave the little guy a show, at Mercer's request." Milo chuckled.

"Your son has a thing for my truck." Cole folded his arms. "Adorable kid. Looks a lot like his mom."

"Thanks." Renee took her son's free hand, and her grandfather released the other one. A smile lit her lovely brown eyes. "Mercer is my everything." She bent down to kiss her son's temple. "We'd better get inside before Gran comes looking for us."

"I'd hoped to get a look at Bea's house," Milo said.

"Why don't we tour the house after lunch?" Cole suggested. "I'm helping Ren with her place today, so I'll be around."

"Mighty generous of you to stick around to help, son." Milo clamped a hand on Cole's shoulder. "This independent granddaughter of mine won't let Janice and me help her. I'm glad she's allowing you to give her a hand."

"You and Gran *are* helping me." Renee slipped an arm through her grandfather's. "There aren't many people in the world I'd trust with my baby. I appreciate knowing he's safe with you while I get everything prepared for us here."

Cole hung back, feeling like an intruder on their family moment.

He owed Milo and Renee more than he could ever articulate. So he wasn't about to do *anything* that might threaten his relationship with either of them. Kissing Renee was a huge mistake.

He was glad Renee was back. Glad they were slowly rebuilding their friendship. But flirting with Ren and leading her on—even though that hadn't been his intention—had blown up their friendship back then. He was supposed to be older and wiser this time around, so he needed to act like it and not screw things up again. Besides, this was business. They were barely a week into this, and already he'd allowed things to get too personal.

Don't forget why you're doing this.

Renee wanted to continue her family's legacy. But his legacy was at stake, too. And no matter what, Ren would have her Aunt Wilhelmina's house and farm. If he was awarded the rest of the Lockwood property, he'd sell her Bea's house and land, too.

She'd have plenty of space for her organic farm.

Cole's phone buzzed with a text message from his foreman on the restaurant project. The man's question could probably be resolved with a quick phone call. But after their kiss and all of the unsettling thoughts turning over in Cole's head, it felt like a good time to create some distance and get his mind right.

"Everything okay, son?" Milo asked.

"Yes, but there's something I need to handle." Cole hated being less than honest with the old man.

"But Janice prepared lunch. You know how much you love her smothered pork chops." The old man chuckled.

Milo wasn't wrong. Cole's mouth watered just thinking of Ms. Janice's delicious smothered pork chops.

"I'll be back in a couple of hours. Save me a plate?"

Milo's frown indicated that he wasn't buying his story. But he didn't challenge him. "All right, son. If you just have to go right now, we won't keep you."

"I realize how busy you are, Cole. So if you can't come back—" Renee was saying.

"I promised to help, and I will. Just as soon as I handle this."

Cole said his goodbyes and got into his truck. He needed a little distance and to put things into perspective. Then he'd return and help Renee, like he'd promised. And he'd keep in mind that they were friends and nothing more.

Nine

Renee loaded more of the books in her aunt's library into boxes, sorting them based on whether she wanted to keep them, donate them or sell them. She picked up an e-reader she'd gifted her great-aunt nearly a decade before. Like the cordless telephone, it was still in the box, unopened. She wiped the dust off, dropped it in the donate box and sneezed.

"Bless you," Cole said, startling her.

She nearly stumbled over the boxes stacked on the floor. "Cole, what are you doing here?"

"I told you I was coming back. You didn't believe me?"

"Let's just say I figured you had something…or *someone*," she murmured under her breath, "to do."

"I did have something to do. And no, it wasn't a

date—" He made it clear he'd heard her snide remark. "But I said I'd be back, and I'm a man of my word. So I'm here."

Maybe he was a man of his word now, but he hadn't been back then. Cole had made her believe he was going to ask her out in high school, by dropping lines like, *Maybe we should go to prom together.* He'd carefully avoided making a commitment while keeping her hopeful and anticipating his invitation.

Cole hadn't been the first jock or rich kid she'd tutored. So she'd been foolish to take those musings seriously. It was Manipulative Hot Boy Tactics 101. Dangle the carrot of a relationship in front of the lonely, undatable girl and watch her twist like a pretzel and run herself ragged trying to catch up to it.

Spoiler alert: it *never* happened.

No matter how fast you ran, no matter how thin you got. Even if you got the expensive makeover—a new hairstyle, all new clothing, contacts, expensive skin care and expert makeup tips—as she had at her former mother-in-law's behest. In the end, she was still that same geeky girl inside. It had taken some time, but she was okay with that. She was proud of who she was and what she'd accomplished in her career.

"I appreciate you honoring your word, Cole, but I'll be fine. I'm sure you have better ways to spend your Saturday afternoon." Renee returned to the shelf and grabbed a handful of books.

"Hey, is something wrong?" Cole put his large hand on her shoulder. "Before I left, we were cool. And now—"

"I shouldn't have kissed you, and I'm sorry. Things

have been really good between us the past week, and then I ruined it." Ren sighed. "I apologize for that."

"Things still are really good between us," Cole insisted.

"You couldn't get out of here fast enough," Ren noted. "Seriously, you skipped out on my grandmother's pork chops—your favorite meal of hers. The Cole Abbott I remember wouldn't have done that, even if his ass was on fire."

"I had some business to take care of at the restaurant my family is opening in the fall." Cole rubbed the back of his neck. "But trust and believe that if I didn't want to be here, Renee, I wouldn't be. You should know enough about me to realize that. Now, how can I help?"

Renee studied Cole's dark eyes, framed by neat brows. He seemed sincere, but she'd fallen for Cole Abbott's charm before.

And look how well that worked out for you.

Ren sighed quietly. She'd had a momentary lapse in judgment. She needed to put her mistake out of her head. Start with a clean slate.

"For starters, let's close these windows." Ren rubbed her arms.

"I've got it." Cole closed the windows that offered a view into his house next door. He frowned. "You're shivering. Here…"

Cole tugged off his Abbott Construction & Development sweatshirt and offered it to her. Beneath it, he wore a blue T-shirt with a picture of a huge muffin on it and the words STUD MUFFIN printed underneath.

Can't accuse the man of false advertising. He does look good enough to eat.

"Take it." His no-nonsense tone sent a chill down her spine and warmed a few other places. "Can't have you getting sick. I plan to win this thing fair and square."

"Thank you." She slipped the sweatshirt over her head. *Great.* Now she'd have to spend the next few hours surrounded by Cole's enticing scent with his company's name splashed across her chest while she tried *not* to think about their kiss.

"Are we boxing up all the books?" Cole turned to study the shelves, but Renee couldn't help studying him. Her gaze was glued to Cole's firm bottom.

Now that's an ass worthy of being chiseled in marble for all eternity.

She sighed quietly. That ass had done its fair share of squats. And she, for one, appreciated it.

"Ren?" Cole glanced over his shoulder at her.

"I…uh…no," she stammered. She stood beside him and studied the bookshelves, too. "I'm deciding which ones to keep, which should be donated and which ones might be worth something. The keepers stay on the shelf. Donations go there. This small stack on the desk I'll have evaluated."

After they created a system, the two of them sorted through the books, mostly in silence.

"Look at this, Ren." Cole set what looked like a stack of books on the table. When he turned it around, she saw that the covers had been hollowed out and attached to a wooden frame.

"Is that a secret compartment?"

"Exactly."

"What was in it?" Ren asked.

Cole climbed the ladder again. He grabbed an armful of leather-bound journals and set them on the coffee table. "These. I think they're your aunt's personal diaries."

"You're kidding." Ren sat on the floor in front of the coffee table and picked up one of the soft, worn journals. She ran her fingers over the faded gold lettering on the front cover. Then she opened the book and traced her fingers across the blue ink and smoothed the pages, yellowed with age and curled at the edges.

It was her aunt's distinct handwriting.

Ren flipped through the pages of the book, reading bits and pieces. But one entry grabbed her attention.

> Today, I begin what I'm calling the Bad Boy Experiment. A secret relationship with Eduardo Cordeiro. I'm not seeking love or marriage. My sole interest in Eduardo is lust—plain and simple. During my summer stay here in Maine, while I'm house-sitting for Aunt Elizabeth, it feels like the right time. Eduardo is a charming ladies' man, but also sweet and kind. He seems like the right man.
>
> When I proposed the idea, Eduardo thought I was joking. Then he was worried about my reputation or that I'd be hurt when things ended. But I've wanted this for a while. I just hadn't met the right man. Until now.
>
> He said he needed to think about it. But yes-

terday, he was waiting on me when I walked into the village to get supplies. We've made arrangements for him to come here late tonight, after the rest of the village is sleeping.

Renee slammed the book shut, her cheeks warm and her heart racing.

"What's wrong?" Cole asked.

"Nothing." She set the journal back on top of the pile. "It just feels wrong, you know. Reading my aunt's most private thoughts. I have no idea what to do with these." She glanced up at Cole. "Do I keep them, or should I burn them?"

"I don't know. But there's something else you should see."

Cole sat on the edge of the coffee table and handed her a large reference book. It was clearly hollow. When she shook it, she could hear the contents of the faux book shifting around inside.

"Is this a book safe?" she asked, suddenly aware of how close Cole was. His scent—the same scent that surrounded her in his soft, warm sweatshirt—teased her senses. She was nearly eye level with his…

"That's what I'm thinking," Cole agreed, clasping his hands between his knees.

Ren's cheeks flamed. Cole had probably seen her checking him out. Not that she'd intended to. But it was *right there*.

Who could blame her?

Ren shifted her attention to the black book in her

lap. She examined it closely. There was a three-digit number lock.

"Please, please, please," she whispered, then tried to open the book. She sighed. "It's locked."

"Wouldn't be much of a safe if it wasn't." Cole winked. "Fortunately, I have about six different tools in my truck that could make quick work of that lock."

Ren pressed her lips together as she turned the idea over in her head. There were literally a thousand possible safe combinations. But wouldn't figuring out the combination be far more satisfying than ripping into this lovely faux book and destroying it with a drill or hacksaw? Besides, if she was meant to see the contents, she'd figure out the combination. If not, she wouldn't. And her aunt's lifetime of secrets would remain safe.

Ren hugged the book to her chest, as if it needed protection from Cole and his power tools. "Thanks for the offer, but I'd prefer to try and figure out the combination."

"It's like a mystery your great-aunt left for you to solve." A soft smile lit Cole's dark eyes. "You always did enjoy a good puzzle."

There was a small fluttering in her chest as she met his gaze. A tiny piece of her heart melted knowing Cole remembered that small detail about her.

"True." She placed the safe in the box with the journals. All of it felt like precious found treasure. "You've been great, Cole. I don't know how I would've gotten through all of this without you."

Cole stared at her without speaking, making Ren feel self-conscious.

She was unsettled. Both by the discovery of her aunt's secret and by the nearness of the man who still managed to turn her knees to jelly and make her heart flutter after all this time.

Maybe I should conduct a bad boy experiment of my own.

It was a ridiculous thought. A recipe for disaster on more levels than she could enumerate.

So why couldn't she stop staring at those full, sensuous, incredibly kissable lips?

Ten

A wave of warmth traveled down Cole's spine as Ren's gaze raked over him, as if she was seeing him for the first time, her eyes filled with heat. It had him feeling things he shouldn't and reliving every moment of their kiss.

"I can transport these books, if you'd like." Cole gestured toward the stacks of boxes.

"Would you, please?" Ren sounded reluctant to ask but he honestly didn't mind. It would take countless trips for her to transport those boxes in her Tesla.

"For you, Ren? Absolutely. I'll start hauling them out to the truck."

Renee thanked him, then scrambled to her feet before he could offer her a hand. She lifted one of the boxes, despite his objections, and quickly dropped it, nearly smashing her foot. “My God, that’s—”

“Heavy?” Cole shoved his hands in his pockets. “That’s what I was trying to tell you. I’ve got a dolly out in the truck. No point in us throwing out our backs for no good reason.”

“Is there ever a good reason to throw out your back?” she asked, then cringed. “Never mind. I stepped right into that one.”

“You kind of did.” He chuckled. “Which means you already know the answer.”

“Have you ever actually…?” She held up a hand. “No, I definitely don’t need to know.”

Cole broke into laughter as he headed toward his truck. “Be back in a flash.”

He returned with a black hand truck and stacked three boxes onto it. It took several trips, but they managed to get all the boxes loaded into his truck without destroying the farmhouse’s rickety back stairs.

“Thanks, Cole. Good night,” Renee said once he’d returned the dolly to his truck.

“You done for the night?” he asked.

“Now that all the books are down and sorted, I’m going to clean and dust the shelves and decide which pieces of furniture to keep. I need to feel like I’ve completed something tonight. It’s just the way my mind works.” She shrugged. “I know you don’t get it, but—”

“I do get it.” He folded his arms. It was her coping mechanism. Ren dealt with the factors in her life she couldn’t control—like her parents being deployed overseas—by controlling the hell out of the things she could.

It was one of the many things about Ren that had been burned into his memory. "Well, let's get to it."

"I've got this." Ren walked toward the house.

He trotted to catch up with her. "Did you honestly think I'd leave you here to finish up on your own?"

"If how frequently your phone keeps buzzing is any indication, someone is looking for you," she said.

She wasn't wrong, There were two missed calls from a casual hookup and text messages from both his mother and sister—each of them trying to set him up with a date for his brothers' upcoming weddings. But he chose not to acknowledge her observation.

"These properties have been abandoned for five years. I'm not leaving you out here all alone at night." He glanced around at the overgrown farmland surrounding them. "Someone could be hiding in those thickets, watching the house."

"You're more worried about this than my grandfather is, Abbott," she noted.

"Don't bet on it."

Milo had asked him to keep an eye on Ren and Mercer once they were all moved in. But he'd asked Cole not to mention it to Ren, who'd already accused him of being overprotective.

"Which reminds me, you should keep this locked when you're here." Cole closed and locked the door behind them.

"Like you said, this place has been sealed up for five years. It needs a good airing out. And before you know it, the days will be getting hotter. I'll have to open the front and back door to get a good cross breeze. I just need to get better screen doors so Mercer doesn't get out. He's obsessed with doors and locks these days."

"I'll have my guys install security screen doors and central air when you're ready." He folded his arms.

"Why do you care so much, Cole?" Renee folded her arms, too.

"Because I do." His face was suddenly warm. He walked past her toward the library. His phone buzzed with another text message from his mother.

Have you considered one of those dating websites, son? Marilyn Diaz's son met a nice girl on one, and now they're getting married.

Cole groaned. His mother and sister were driving him up a wall about who he was going to bring to these weddings. And the first was still several months away.

"And you just assumed I'd hire your company to do the work?" Ren's words brought him back to his current dilemma: trying to get this stubborn woman to accept his help.

"I'm the only person who'd be willing to do the work at cost *and* pass on my bulk discounts. So yeah, I kind of did," he said.

"You're willing to do the work without making a profit, even though we're competing to impress my grandfather?"

"Yes."

"Why?"

Cole narrowed his gaze. "You're familiar with the phrase *don't look a gift horse in the mouth*, right?"

Renee picked up one of the books from the keep pile and fanned through it.

"I guess I'm just not accustomed to someone going the extra mile without there being some ulterior motive."

That was it.

Cole rubbed his chin. If Ren needed to believe that he had to have some selfish motive, he'd give her one. They could make a trade, just as they'd done by helping each other clean out the houses.

She propped a hand on her hip. "You *do* have an ulterior motive."

Cole laughed in response to the shift in Renee's expression. It reminded him of Arnold from the old sitcom *Diff'rent Strokes*, when he'd ask his older brother *What chu talkin' 'bout, Willis?*

"I prefer to think of it as bartering," he said. "Your aunts were farmers. They must've bartered with neighboring farms and other vendors all the time."

"They did. But something tells me this won't just be an innocent, neighborly barter." She eyed him suspiciously.

Did she actually think he needed to trade sex for discount services? *Damn.* He was more than a little insulted by that.

"I need a date. Three, actually. One for Parker and Kayleigh's wedding, one for Max and Quinn's wedding and one for the opening of my family's restaurant later this fall." He ticked each event off on his fingers.

"And you want me to be...what? Your fake girlfriend

or something?" she asked. "I'm a little too busy to be battling clingy exes in the street."

Cole burst into laughter at the image of Ren removing her earrings and greasing her face in preparation for a street fight. Ren laughed, too.

"I'm not asking you to be my fake girlfriend, and there are no clingy exes in my past," he assured her. "So you won't need to fight anyone in the street over me. Though I'm pretty flattered that the only thing holding you back is that you're busy."

"That's *not* what I meant, and you know it." Ren shoved Cole's shoulder playfully.

A wave of warmth settled over him. He'd missed the easy, teasing friendship he and Ren once had. He couldn't help wondering if she missed it, too.

Ren raked her fingers through her messy hair. "So what are you proposing?"

"I'm asking you to be my plus-one for these family events. We'd be going as friends—that's all." He shrugged.

"Don't you have a *friend*—" Ren used air quotes "—for this sort of thing?"

"I did. But since she's marrying my brother in a few months, I'm pretty sure she already has a date to all this stuff—including her own wedding." Cole forced a smile.

"Oh… I see."

Cole didn't miss the pity in Ren's voice. A knot tightened in his gut. He wanted to tell her that he was happy for them. *Really.*

But even in his head, it made him sound pitiful.

Maybe the twinge of envy he felt was less about Max marrying Quinn and more about the fact that he would be the last unmarried Abbott standing. Which was fine, because he wasn't looking for a serious relationship. But still, seeing all his siblings happy and in love, starting families and building futures with their significant others, it had made him think about his own future in ways he hadn't before.

"And you don't want to take any of your other women *friends* because…?"

"I think it's better if I don't… I mean… I…"

"Ahh…" Ren nodded, knowingly. "You don't want to take someone you're involved with to a wedding, lest she get wild ideas about marriage and kids…with you."

Cole prided himself on being open and genuine. But maybe he needed to be a little more mysterious. Then again, his transparency had always been part of his charm. What you saw was what you got. No cat-and-mouse games. No bullshit. Just a little fun and a whole lot of—

"I'll take your silence as confirmation." Renee interrupted his thoughts.

"You haven't answered my question." Cole didn't want to delve any deeper into his commitment issues. They were there. He was aware of them. They'd become old friends.

Renee frowned. "And these dates would be strictly platonic?"

"Absolutely." Cole didn't wait for a response. He climbed the ladder with the furniture spray and a cloth and started dusting.

If he was being honest, his ego was taking a hit. Renee had kissed him. He would've expected her to readily agree to his proposal.

They worked together another hour to dust the shelves and organize the furniture. Finally, Ren locked up the house. Cole walked her to her Tesla. He opened the driver's door and gestured for her to get inside.

Ren tossed her small purse into the passenger seat, then pushed the sleeves of his sweatshirt up her arms. "I'll wash your shirt and return it."

"Keep it." The thing practically swallowed her. But there was something about seeing Ren in his oversize shirt that warmed his chest. "Got plenty."

"Thank you again, Cole." Ren propped her folded arms on top of the door. "For everything you've done tonight and for your generous offer." Ren glanced back at the old house fondly, then gazed up at him. "I accept the proposal to be your plus-one."

"Great." He responded a little too quickly, his voice a little too high.

Ren giggled. "It'll be nice to see your family again. Your mom was always so sweet."

"That reminds me..." Cole snapped his fingers. "My mother asked me to invite you and Mercer to the birthday party for my nephew, Davis, and Benji and Sloane's twins. The kids would love to meet Mercer."

"Thank you." Ren tucked her hair behind her ear. "But I don't know if we should. Mercer doesn't take well to everyone."

"He took to me." Cole studied Ren's face. There was something else she wasn't saying.

"He did," Ren agreed, seemingly surprised. "But the truth is I don't want him to feel…out of place." Ren shifted her gaze from his and wrapped her arms around herself.

"Because he's nonverbal?" The pained look on Ren's face made his chest ache. He wanted to punch her ex in the face for leaving her and Mercer to fend for themselves.

"That and his stimming. The constant little sounds he makes and how he runs in circles sometimes. They're self-soothing behaviors some autistic children use to manage their emotions or cope with anxiety," she clarified in response to his look of confusion. "And no, I'm not embarrassed by any of it. But it sometimes makes people uncomfortable. And *that* makes Mercer uncomfortable." Ren sighed heavily. "We went through that with my ex's family. I won't put my son through that again."

"It won't be like that, Ren. I promise." Cole put a hand on her shoulder, his heart breaking for Ren and Mercer. How could her ex and her in-laws have acted like that? "I know it feels easier to just avoid people rather than giving them a chance. But you came back here for a new start. You and Mercer should meet people. Become part of the community. After all, everyone in town is a potential customer for the farm. And my family is opening a new farm-to-table restaurant. Quinn—my future sister-in-law—is working with my mom to ensure all of the food is locally sourced. It wouldn't hurt to start building a relationship with both of them."

"And they'll both be there," Ren said more to herself than him. She sighed. "Okay. We'll come. And now that my social calendar is full, I'd like to go back to my grandparents' place, take a hot shower, then snuggle up to my kid and go to sleep for the night. Thanks, Cole." She lifted onto her toes and kissed his cheek. Then she got into her Tesla and pulled onto the unlit, rural road.

Cole climbed into his TRX and started it. His hand drifted to the cheek Ren had just kissed.

He heaved a sigh and shifted the truck into Drive.

Cole still had a gooey, soft center when it came to Renee Lockwood. But regardless of how good Renee looked, smelled, tasted…his focus was on his next building project. And he wouldn't let anyone—not even Ren—get in the way of that.

Eleven

Renee collapsed onto the sofa in her aunt's old library, which she'd converted into her office. She propped her feet on the arm of the couch, draped an arm over her face and tried to catch her breath.

Aunt Wilhelmina's old house now officially belonged to her, and she and Mercer had moved in a little more than a week ago. But the sudden change in their daily routine had been a difficult adjustment for her son. He'd been cranky and miserable all day, and Renee had spent the past hour on the verge of tears, trying to decipher exactly what it was her frustrated little boy wanted. Now that he was finally down for his nap, she could use a power nap of her own to recover.

Renee was exhausted, her head was throbbing and she was pretty sure there were bits of banana in her hair.

All she'd eaten was a handful of Mercer's Cheerios earlier that morning in an attempt to get him to eat them.

She reveled in the stillness of the room and the absolute silence throughout the house. For the first time today, she could hear herself think. More importantly, she needed this space of solitude to work on her plans for the farm and make phone calls to potential vendors.

Ren glanced around the room. The place was slowly coming along. Her office, painted sea-foam green, felt brighter but also warm and cozy now. On an accent wall painted a bolder, deeper shade of green, she'd hung an array of family photos, many of which she'd retrieved from her aunt's collection.

She'd gotten rid of a lot of the oversize furniture but kept the antique wooden desk—the piece she most associated with her aunt. The room flowed better now and appealed to her minimalist aesthetic. But it was also safer for Mercer. The more spacious layout would permit him to make a circuit around the coffee table or sofa without hurting himself.

Renee rolled onto her side with her arm folded beneath her head. She set a ten-minute timer and shut her eyes. She was close to drifting asleep when she heard a faint rumbling sound. Was that thunder or a truck rumbling down her street?

She rolled onto her back, her eyes open, and listened carefully. Everything was quiet. Perhaps she'd imagined it. She closed her eyes again. But then she heard what was definitely the rumbling of a vehicle engine, and the low thump of bass from Bob Marley's "Could You Be Loved."

Renee rose from the couch and walked over to the window. A white moving truck was slowly backing into Cole's driveway, making a beeping sound. When the truck came to a halt, three men hopped out, laughing and joking. Moments later, Cole's truck pulled into her driveway.

Renee ducked away from the window, hoping Cole hadn't seen her. There was the slam of his truck door, and then a knock at her kitchen door.

She froze and considered not answering. It'd been a month since she had kissed Cole. Ren cringed remembering it. She'd always been low-key and reserved. And she'd never, *ever* made the first move on a guy. So what had possessed her to kiss him?

Ren hadn't spoken to Cole since their encounter. He'd sent her a text with the info on the events she'd committed to attending. And they'd waved to each other in passing. But that was it.

Why did he have to show up at her door today when she looked an absolute mess? She was wearing her old, beat-up glasses, a cruddy pair of gray sweatpants permanently stained with finger paints and food and, to top it all off, the sweatshirt Cole had loaned her.

Cole knocked again.

Shit.

If he kept knocking, he'd wake Mercer from his nap. As much as she adored her little boy, she valued her two free hours in the middle of the day. Besides, if Merce didn't get his nap, he'd be even crankier the rest of the day, and no one wanted that.

Ren considered taking off Cole's sweatshirt but she

wore only a bra beneath it. She groaned quietly. She would choose today, of all days, to look like a raging dumpster fire and to be wearing Cole's sweatshirt while doing it.

She huffed, then hurried to the door before Cole could knock again.

Renee swept back the loose hair that had escaped her half-ass ponytail. She opened the door just enough to show her face.

While she looked like a hot mess, Cole looked… ridiculously handsome. How did the man manage to do that in a simple pocketed T-shirt bearing his company's logo and a pair of broken-in but expensive jeans? Maybe it was the dark shades. They lent an air of mystery, since she couldn't see his eyes.

"Hey," she finally said.

"Hey." Cole's mouth curved in a slow smirk and one brow shifted upward.

Was he amused because she looked like a disaster? Or because she was peering out of a small crack in the door with one eye, in an effort to hide the fact that she looked like a disaster?

"Not sure if you just don't want to be bothered right now or if I should ask you to blink twice if you're being held hostage." Cole peered over her head into the kitchen.

"I'm fine." Ren sighed, opening the door wider. She tried to ignore the flames licking the sides of her face as she died a slow death of embarrassment. "I laid Mercer down a few minutes ago, and I'm trying desperately to make sure he stays asleep. As you can see, it's been a rough day." She indicated her stained and wrinkled outfit. "Let's just say this nap is essential to his sanity and mine."

"Sorry, I didn't consider that Little Man might be taking a nap." Cole rubbed the back of his head. "I came to ask if it'd be okay for me to park in your driveway while the guys are moving my stuff in. I'm expecting a few deliveries today, so I wanted to leave room for the drivers to go in and out."

"Yeah…sure. I'm not going anywhere or expecting anyone, so help yourself."

Cole thanked her but didn't move. "Told you that sweatshirt looked good on you."

"Uh…thanks?" Ren self-consciously pushed up the too-long sleeves. "Is there anything else?"

"No, but I definitely don't want to wake your son." Cole rubbed his beard. "So why don't I give the guys a break? I'll treat them to a long lunch. Then we can start moving once Mercer is up from his nap."

"You're going to halt work for two hours to accommodate my son's nap?" Ren asked in disbelief.

"My sister-in-law, Savannah, adores my niece and nephew, and she's an amazing mom. But she looks forward to those daily naps. You're raising Mercer alone. I'd imagine that's especially true for you."

"Yes." Ren wrapped her arms around herself and nodded. "It's been more challenging than I expected to get work done when it's just the two of us here." She hated admitting that her plan already had a fatal flaw. She expected Cole to gloat, but he didn't.

"Then I'll let the fellas know before they get started. Text me when the little guy is up."

It seemed like a small thing, Cole adjusting his day for the sake of her and her son. He was just being a decent neighbor, after all. So why were her eyes stinging with tears of gratitude?

Perhaps because he'd offered the concession without her asking for it. Such thoughtful consideration had come to mean the world to her.

Ren stepped onto the back porch and called quietly to Cole, who'd trotted down the stairs.

"Yes?"

"Thank you. I didn't mean to come off as…" She sighed, running her fingers through her messy hair. "I'm sleep-deprived and a little hangry."

His mouth curved in a soft smile that made Ren's heart melt. He nodded, then jogged over to deliver the news to the movers.

Renee returned to the sofa in her office because she really did need that nap. But as she lay there staring at the ceiling, she couldn't fall asleep. Every time she closed her eyes, all she could see was that damn smile of Cole's.

Twelve

Cole tapped quietly on the window of Ren's office. There was no answer, so he tried again.

Ren came to the window, her beautiful face twisted in a frown as she pushed her glasses up her adorable nose. She obviously didn't appreciate the additional interruption. But even annoyed and completely disheveled, Ren was gorgeous.

He held up a box of pizza and pointed to it.

Ren twisted her mouth before nodding and gesturing for him to go to the back door.

Cole trotted to the back porch, where she was waiting with the door open. She held a finger to her mouth, indicating he should be quiet, and for some reason he couldn't help focusing on her full lips or get the visual of Ren as a stern schoolteacher out of his head.

Get it together, man. Ren is off-limits.

A fresh, lemony scent filled the room. The kitchen floor shone, as if recently mopped.

"Hold this." Cole handed her the pizza, then loosened the laces on his Timbs and toed them off.

"You brought us pizza?" Ren held up the box.

"And a lunch date." Cole grinned, stepping inside. "If you don't mind some company."

Her deadpan expression indicated she had zero interest in entertaining anyone. But she forced a smile anyway.

"Sure. Company would be nice. That is if you don't mind eating with someone who looks like they've been dragged through hell." She glanced down at her sweats—including the sweatshirt he'd loaned her, which was currently dotted with various stains and little handprints.

Why did that make her even more adorable?

This woman was seriously messing with his head. Making him feel all warm and fuzzy when warm and fuzzy definitely wasn't his thing. He preferred to feel hot and bothered. Then again, Ren managed to make him feel that, too.

"You look like a busy mom." Cole shrugged. "But you'd look good wearing a paper bag, Ren. So don't sweat it. Tell you what. You've had a rough day. Why don't you let me serve you?"

Ren raked her fingers through her hair. "You want to serve me lunch?"

"It's pizza, Ren. Minimal effort required." He smirked. "But yeah. Where can I wash my hands?"

She blinked, her mouth opening, then snapping shut again. "This way," she said finally as she led him down a narrow hallway.

"Ren...you have... I mean there's—"

"What?" Ren stopped in front of the door of the half bathroom and turned to face him.

Cole turned her back around and carefully peeled a half-eaten pink Starburst off her perfectly round and exceedingly plump ass. He handed the candy to her.

Ren's eyes widened. "That little boy. I swear. He must've found my candy stash. *That's* why he was so hyper and irritable today. Sugar, especially large amounts, throws him off." She stepped inside the bathroom and tossed the partially eaten candy into the toilet and flushed. "You've just solved the mystery of my awful morning."

She washed and dried her hands, then gestured that the sink was all his before disappearing down the hall.

When he returned to the kitchen, she was sliding slices of pizza onto their plates.

"I'm supposed to be serving you, remember?" Cole raised an eyebrow. "I see you're still not great at following instructions."

"Actually, I'm excellent at following instructions." She shoved her lopsided glasses up the bridge of her nose. "It's direction I don't take very well. As in when two men—you being one of them—tell me I can't and shouldn't do this on my own." She gestured around them.

"Never said you couldn't. And neither of us doubt your ability." He accepted a plate from her and set it on the table. “Milo and I just want to make sure you know exactly what you’ve signed up for here. Honestly? Your grandfather is a genius,” Cole declared. “Plenty of folks move here from the city with aspirations of starting a little organic farm or raising free-range chickens. It’s not nearly as glamorous as reality TV makes it seem when you’re standing ankle deep in cow manure.”

“Dude!” Renee cringed with a mouth full of pizza. “I’m trying to eat here.”

“My bad.” He chuckled. “My point is that most people don’t stick with it, and they often come out of their little fantasy experiment with substantial losses. You gotta admit, making you invest six months into converting this smaller plot to a working farm first is a great way to prove to him and to yourself that you’re in this for the long haul. And if you decide this isn’t what you want…there’s no shame in that, Ren.”

“I have no intention of changing my mind.” Renee regarded him suspiciously. She wiped her hands. “I don’t make snap decisions. I’ve been thinking about and planning this for a year. So if this impromptu luncheon was designed to convince me to give up—”

“That isn’t why I came.” He set his pizza down, wishing he’d kept his mouth shut. “You hadn’t eaten, and you’ve had a tough day. I wanted to feed you and maybe make your day a little better, like you did so many times for me when I had a shitty day in high school. That’s all.”

Ren’s gaze softened. “I didn’t think you remembered any of that.”

“Did you really think I’d forget you making my favorite cookies in geometric shapes and only letting me have one when I got a problem right?" Cole chuckled, his chest warming at the memory of those afternoons they spent together in winter and spring of senior year. "Despite the fact that there was math involved—which I actually do use on jobs, just like you said I would—those were some of my most cherished high school memories." He placed a hand on his chest.

"If doing math with me at my grandparents' kitchen table was one of your best high school memories, your high school experience was even sadder than mine." She nibbled on her pizza. "So forgive me if I have a hard time believing that."

"It's true. Scout's honor." Cole raised his hand in a three-fingered salute.

"Weren't you tossed out of the Scouts?" Renee raised a brow.

"I quit, actually. Too many rules. But completely irrelevant."

Ren rolled her eyes.

"You still don't believe me." Cole took another bite of his pizza. He'd gotten one half wall-to-wall meat, the other side plain cheese. Just in case Mercer was as picky about what he wanted on his pizza as Blake's and Benji's kids were. "Why?"

Ren frowned, shifting her gaze from his.

"Go ahead." He already knew what she was going to say. But she needed to say the words to him aloud and he deserved to hear them. No matter how blistering they might be.

"What do you want me to say, Cole?" She walked

over to the cabinet and grabbed two glasses, filling them with filtered water from a pitcher in the fridge.

"Say whatever is on your mind and be honest."

"You're reminiscing over the past like we were the best of friends. And for a time, I was foolish enough to believe maybe we were. But then you were flirting, and I flirted back." Her eyes filled with fresh pain. "You *implied* we should go to prom together. I turned down other offers because I was so sure you were going to ask me. But you didn't. I felt like such a fool for believing someone like you would want to go to prom with someone like me."

Ren's voice trailed off. She leaned against the wall in the archway between the kitchen and dining room.

Cole came to stand in front of her, shoving his hands in his pockets. His chest ached with guilt and regret.

"I'm sorry if I hurt you, Ren. I genuinely intended to ask you to the prom but—" Cole had wanted to apologize to Ren for so long. Yet he hadn't been prepared to revisit the insecurity and self-doubt he'd felt back then.

"But *what*, Cole?"

Her dark eyes demanded an answer, and he wouldn't deny her the satisfaction of finally knowing the truth.

He could still hear the words of his buddy when he'd told him that he'd planned to ask Ren to the prom.

Your math tutor? Seriously, man? No way that girl is into you. She's a fucking genius. Meanwhile, your family won't even give you a job sweeping at the distillery 'cause you refuse to go to college. What would you two even talk about? Look, every girl loves a bad boy, especially a rich one. That's what she's interested in.

"Cole?" Ren said again.

"I…uh…" He rubbed the scruff on his jaw.

"You were the popular, ever-cool Cole Abbott, and you were embarrassed to be seen at the prom with the nerdy, sci-fi-obsessed bookworm whose wardrobe was a disaster." Ren shrugged. "I get it. It was snobbish and rude, but we were just kids. You obviously aren't that guy anymore. So let's just forget about it."

None of that was true. It was Ren who was too good for him. He opened his mouth to tell her as much, but the words seemed to get stuck in his throat.

"Maybe you're right," Ren continued. "I was still holding a grudge over the entire thing. That was silly after all this time. I accept your apology. Truce?" Ren opened her arms for a hug.

Cole nodded, angry with himself for not leveling with her. He wrapped his arms around Renee, resting his chin atop her head. "I hope we can be friends again. Because I honestly do miss those days at your grandparents' kitchen table."

"Me, too." Ren stepped out of his embrace and swiped the back of her finger beneath her eyes. There was a pained smile on her sweet face. "Of all the places I've lived, Magnolia Lake is the only one that's ever really felt like home. And you are the closest friend I had here." She wiped the damp corners of her eyes and gave a nervous laugh. "It would be nice if we could salvage that friendship."

"Regardless of your grandfather's final decision?" He hated to break the hazy bubble of nostalgia and friendship, but he needed to know.

"Regardless of what Grandad decides." Ren extended her hand.

Cole accepted it, holding it a beat longer than he probably should've. Electricity sparked in his palm and seemed to travel up his arm.

Had she felt it, too? Or was it all in his head?

"Ma, ma, ma!" Mercer's voice was accompanied by the sound of his bare feet slapping against the wooden stairs and the thump of a toy he was dragging down one step at a time.

"Hey there, sweetheart. You're up from your nap already." Ren slipped her hand from Cole's, then opened her arms to her son as she stooped to hug him.

Mercer wrapped one of his wiry little arms around her neck. Then he gazed up at Cole, his smile widening. "Vroom!"

Cole pointed a thumb to his chest. "Me?"

"Vroom," Mercer said again, clutching the toy truck he'd dragged down the stairs.

"He loves trucks, and apparently he remembers yours." Ren stood behind her son with her hands on his little shoulders. "Say hello to Mr. Cole, sweetie."

"Mr. Cole? God, that makes me sound old," he groused.

"Vroom!" Mercer's smile was big enough to light up an entire city.

"I much prefer that." Cole chuckled. He squatted so he was eye level with Mercer. "Hey there, little guy. It's good to see you again. I brought pizza."

"Eat!" Mercer dropped his truck and headed for the kitchen.

Cole laughed as he watched the little boy climb into his booster seat at the kitchen table.

Ren followed her son to the kitchen and pulled out colorful plates and cups. She put a slice of cheese pizza on Mercer's plate and cut it into smaller pieces. "You should probably let the movers know they can get started." Ren poured water into a blue kiddie cup.

"Oh, yeah. I should." Cole went toward the door, then stopped and turned back to Renee and Mercer. "Actually, I could just call them and let them know, if you wouldn't mind me hanging out here to finish lunch with you two."

Ren smiled. "That would be nice."

Something about Ren's smile had always done things to him, but never more than right now. If he'd been smart, he would've taken it as a warning to turn and run.

But instead, he sank back onto his chair, made a quick call to the movers and spent the next hour enjoying his time with Renee and Mercer.

Thirteen

"Nervous about your date with Cole?" Renee's mother, Evelyn, glanced up from buttoning Mercer's purple plaid shirt. She'd come to spend the week with them and help with the house.

"It's not a date, Mama." Ren fussed with her hair in the mirror of the front hall.

"You're going to tell me that a children's birthday party typically calls for this much primping?"

"What?" Ren tugged her hair over one shoulder and met her mother's teasing grin. "You're the one who said I should make self-care a priority."

"I was thinking a hot-stone massage and a facial or something." Her mother laughed. "But a little bad boy experiment of your own…that sounds even better."

"A—I told you, there is nothing going on between

me and Cole. B—don't make me sorry I told you about Aunt Wilhelmina's diary." Ren pointed a finger at her mother, then smoothed down her skirt, hoping she wasn't overdressed.

"You can keep telling yourself there's nothing going on. But I've seen the way you two look at each other. And that giddy laugh of yours whenever Cole is around… Seriously, sweetheart, the only person you're fooling here is yourself." Her mother clucked her tongue. "And if there isn't anything going on between you two…maybe there should be."

"Mom, what on earth has gotten into you?" Ren brushed past her mother in search of Mercer's shoes. "I'm not interested in getting involved again. I was married to the rogue son from the wealthy family, remember? It's completely overrated. Besides, what happened to the woman who always lectured me about not letting some knucklehead boy sidetrack me from my goals and aspirations? In case you've forgotten, I'm starting a new business here. Between Mercer and the farm, I'm too busy for a relationship."

"Well, you've certainly made time to rekindle your friendship with Cole. And he's made it his business to help you get the farm started—even though it isn't in his best interest to do so." Her mother retrieved Mercer's shoes from beneath the sofa and held them up. She chased him down and sat on the sofa with Mercer on her lap.

Ren sank onto the sofa beside her mother and put on Mercer's shoes. When she was done, Mercer ran off. She could only hope he kept his shoes on. Her son hated footwear.

"Of course, I haven't forgotten what you're doing here, and I admire you for it, sweetheart." Her mother squeezed her hand. "It's a worthwhile ambition, but it's going to be tough. Tougher than you seem to realize. You're a selfless, dedicated mother. I applaud the sacrifices you're making to give Mercer the best life possible. All I'm saying is that maybe Aunt Willie was on to something with this idea of having a temporary fling."

"Mom!" Renee honestly couldn't believe her mother was saying this. Since her parents' divorce, her dad had remarried and seemed reasonably content. But her mother was living her best, sexually liberated single life.

"Fine. We won't talk about it." Her mother collected some of Mercer's toys and dropped them into the toy chest in Ren's office. "Have you considered my offer to keep Mercer for a few weeks? It'd give you a chance to get some things done around here. You're on the clock, and there's still so much to do."

"It's a generous offer. But I don't know. Merce has never been away from me for that long."

"You don't know if he can handle the separation?"

"I'm not sure *I* can handle it." Ren sighed.

"You'll both be fine." Her mother draped an arm over her shoulder. "We'll only be an hour away in Knoxville. If Mercer doesn't adapt well, I promise to bring him back. But you could use the break. You have lots to do, and I know it isn't easy when Mercer is underfoot."

Her mother wasn't wrong, but she wasn't about to admit it.

"Vroom! Vroom! Vroom!" Mercer ran out of her office and toward the back door; his shoes and socks had been discarded.

"Mercer!" His grandmother went hunting for his socks and shoes. Ren couldn't help laughing.

The distinctive knock at her back door instantly elicited a deep smile.

Cole.

Mercer must've seen him walking along the path toward their house from her office window. The window where he often stood waving to Cole when he returned home each evening.

Ren stood, smoothing down her skirt. She sucked in a deep breath and headed for the back door.

"Definitely a date," her mother called after her in a loud whisper.

Maybe her mother was right, but it seemed best to ignore her mom and the little voice in her head that agreed that this was totally a date.

Cole watched Ren as she chatted with his mother, Savannah and his sister, Zora, who seemed more pregnant every time he saw her again.

Honestly, it was still weird to realize that his baby sister was married—to her lifetime best friend, no less—and that she would be a mother in a few short months. During which, two of his four brothers would be getting married. Thank God for the grandkids, or all of Iris Abbott's effort and energy would be devoted to marrying him off, too.

"So I hear you have a new bestie." Quinn handed him a beer from the cooler and stood beside him.

"Why, you jealous?" He smirked, accepting the beer and twisting off the top.

"Only the tiniest bit." Quinn peered between her thumb and forefinger and laughed. "Because though I lost a close friend, I gained a brother." She nudged him with her elbow. "By the way, when your new bestie isn't watching her adorable little boy, she's got her eyes on you. Is there something you need to tell us?"

"Not you, too." Cole frowned, then sipped his beer. "Ren and I are friends. That's all."

"Does she know that?" Quinn sipped her peach brandy. It was the product line his family's distillery had collaborated on with Bazemore Orchards—owned by Quinn's grandfather, one of Grandpa Joe's closest friends.

"Yes, *Peaches*, she does." Cole emphasized Quinn's childhood nickname, which she only let her grandfather and fiancé get away with using.

Quinn elbowed him in the side and pointed a finger. "Don't make me jump you."

"All right, all right." He held up his hands in surrender.

"But seriously, Cole," Quinn said once their laughter had died down. "Maybe it isn't more than just friends for you. But the way the two of them look at you… There's definitely something more there for them. I'd hate to see anyone get hurt."

"Why does everyone assume I'm going to hurt Ren?" He'd already gotten versions of this speech from his mother and Zora. It was disappointing to hear it from Quinn, too.

"Actually, it's *you* I'm worried about." Quinn gave him a warm smile. "You're a good guy, Cole. And you're softer in the center than you like to think you are. That little boy adores you." She nodded to where Mercer was bouncing on his toes while Kayleigh's dog, Cricket, danced on her paws, seemingly in sync with him.

"Because I'm a big kid, too." Cole shrugged as if it were no big deal and sipped more of his beer. "I'm the fun uncle, and I take my job seriously."

"Maybe." Quinn sipped her drink. "Or maybe it's because you get each other and you really care about him and his mom, and Mercer is perceptive enough to recognize that."

Cole swallowed hard, her words running through his head. But he couldn't form a response.

Quinn smiled softly. "I'd better go. Looks like Sloane could use help with the cake."

Cole drained the rest of his beer, unable to shake off Quinn's observation. He did feel a kinship with Mercer. He'd struggled with a language-based learning disability, while Mercer's was a developmental one. Still, he did understand that struggle. And maybe the reason he'd fallen so hard for the kid so quickly was because he understood a little of what he must be going through. Seeing how damn hard his mother fought for him made him respect and adore her, too.

But respect, adoration and even friendship did not necessarily equate to a relationship. So yes, they were just friends. He was a friend who also just happened to admire her perfect bottom and the full breasts having a child had evidently gifted Ren.

"See that? That was definitely not a friendly look." Zora poked Cole in the arm, her other hand resting on her ever-growing belly.

"Are y'all tag teaming me?" He tossed his beer bottle in a nearby can.

"Someone has to." Zora shrugged. "But what I wanted to ask is—are you absolutely certain you're bringing Renee to Parker and Kayleigh's wedding?"

"Yes, why?"

"Savannah and I want to invite her to Kayleigh's wedding shower in a couple of weeks. But if we invite her and then you decide to bring someone else… *awkward*."

Okay, so maybe that had happened that one time. His bad. But at least he'd learned his lesson. That was exactly why he didn't bring people he was involved with to family functions anymore.

"You're good," Cole insisted. "Ask her. She'll try to wiggle out of it. Not because she doesn't want to attend, but because she's a little shy and afraid she's intruding somehow. Let her know you really want her to be there, and she won't say no."

"You know her pretty well." Zora's voice had softened, as had her expression. "Whatever this is, bro…" She waved a hand in his direction and smiled. "It looks good on you."

"Don't start again, Zo."

"I know you love playing the role of the family badass—" she indicated his Badass Mama's Boy T-shirt visible beneath his open button-down "—but we both know you're probably the most sensitive out of all of us."

"I am *not* fucking sensitive." Cole pointed a finger, which only made Zora laugh.

"Okay. Bighearted. That better?" Zora slipped her arm through his. "There's nothing wrong with that, Cole. I happen to adore bighearted men. Got one of my own." She smiled at Dallas, who was holding his niece, Remi. "Seems Renee appreciates a bighearted man, too."

When Cole glanced over at Ren, she was staring at him. She tucked her hair behind her ear and leaned down to say something to Mercer, who was chasing bubbles across the yard.

Why was it that every time he met that gaze and soft smile, his heart felt like it was growing in his chest? Like he was tumbling in a dream? Maybe Zora was right. He was sensitive as fuck. Which was why he normally avoided this kind of entanglement. But he was already in too deep.

"You're the only one who seems to think I have a big heart." Cole nodded toward where Max stood with his arm looped around Quinn's waist.

"Max treats you like the family asshole because that's what you want him to think." Zora glanced up at him, sadness in her eyes. "Because that's easier than being vulnerable and telling him or Dad the truth."

"And what is the truth, Zo?" He frowned.

"That how they treated you wasn't fair. That it didn't take into account who you are. Your sensibilities. The learning differences you struggled with." His sister's eyes were filled with compassion. "You have a unique way of seeing the world, and working at King's Finest wasn't the best use for it."

"I don't need validation from Max," Cole said. "Or Dad or Gramps, for that matter."

"Then why are you always trying to prove something that no one but you gives a damn about?" Zora slipped her arm from his and rubbed her back. "From where I'm standing, you care an awful lot about proving them wrong. But you don't have to. Dad and Grandad are immensely proud of you, Cole. We all are."

"Then why does Max bring up me not working for KFD every chance he gets?"

"Maybe Max still doesn't understand why you didn't want to work for the family. But he does admire what you've accomplished." Zora ran her fingers through her shoulder-length two-strand twists and tugged them over one shoulder. "So instead of always trying to piss him off, why don't you try talking to him for a change?"

"So this thing with me and Max is all my fault?"

"There's enough blame to go around, believe me," Zora acknowledged. "But someone needs to make the first step. All I'm saying is…why can't that be you?"

Cole groaned and looked over at Max begrudgingly. "Fine. I'll talk to him."

"When?"

His sister was relentless. "We just had a moment here. Can't we just celebrate that for a minute?"

"Would you mind giving him a bath? I'll be up to read him a story shortly," Ren said.

"Leave story time to me." Her mother grinned, glancing between the two of them. "It'll give us a chance to practice for when he stays with me."

They watched as her mother ascended the stairs with Mercer on her shoulder.

"It's great your mother was able to come and help out. How long is she staying?"

"Another few days. But she'd like to keep Mercer in Knoxville for a week once or twice a month so I can get some things done around here."

"You okay letting Little Man go away for an entire week?" Cole asked.

It tugged at her chest that Cole understood her anxiety about being separated from her son. It wasn't that she didn't trust her mother to keep Mercer. She had difficulty trusting *anyone* with watching her fearless little daredevil.

"Not really, but it would help me get back on schedule."

"Then you should do it." Cole gave her a reassuring smile. "Evelyn will take good care of him."

Before she could respond, her mother hurried down the steps, clutching her robe. "I don't want you to panic, but I can't find Mercer."

"He was with you a few minutes ago, and he hasn't come downstairs. He has to be up there." Renee did her best not to freak out. It wasn't as if Mercer was wandering the overgrown fields. "He's probably fallen asleep under his bed or mine."

"I checked under his bed. He's not there. And he can't be in your room. Your door is locked," Evelyn said, panicked.

"I didn't lock my door. I didn't even realize that the lock on that door worked." *Now* she was panicking. Mercer had accidentally locked himself in her room. She bounded up the stairs two at a time, with her mother on her heels.

Ren got on her knees and peeked through the skeleton keyhole of the old door. The room was dark, so she couldn't tell for sure whether Mercer was in there or not. He'd probably crawled into her bed and fallen asleep, so she didn't want to bang on the door and startle him.

"I swear, sweetheart, I turned my back for one minute to run his bathwater and find him some pajamas. When I went to put him in the tub—"

"It's okay." Ren squeezed her mother's arms. "I'm not blaming you. Mercer is an active, curious kid. He's here, and we'll find him. But not if the two of us stand here panicking, all right?"

Ren could see the moment her mom shifted from a concerned grandmother to a retired army officer. She held back her shoulders and tipped her chin.

"We need to pick the lock," her mother said.

"Can you pick this old lock?" Ren asked. "Because I can't."

"Then we need to break the door down."

"This door is solid pine. It'll take a lot more strength than either of us can muster."

"I beg your pardon." Her mother put a hand on her

hip. "I might be retired, but I still work out. I'm stronger than I look."

"Yeah, and the last time you went all G.I. Jane, you threw out your back. We can't afford to have that happen again," Ren reminded her.

"Fine. Cole should be able to handle it." Her mother turned around.

It was the first they'd noticed that Cole hadn't followed them up the stairs.

"Cole?" Ren walked toward the stairs. Her son wasn't Cole's responsibility. But as fond as he and Mercer were of each other, she couldn't believe he'd just walk away without trying to help.

"He probably went to his truck to get a tool. I'll check."

Her mother hurried down the stairs.

Suddenly, the light in her bedroom shone from beneath the door, and there was the sound of the door being unlocked.

"Mercer?" Ren's heart was racing.

The doorknob slowly turned, and the door creaked open.

"Cole?" There were half a dozen questions in her head. "Did you find Mercer?"

"He's not in the bed or in the closet. I've already checked." His brows were furrowed with worry. "But we'll find him. Like you said, he has to be up here some—"

"Wait." Ren covered Cole's mouth with her hand. "Listen."

"Is that snoring?" Cole asked.

She nodded. "He's definitely here. You're sure you checked the closet?"

"Positive. There's no way he's in there." Cole stooped, then got on his hands and knees. He lifted the bed skirt and peeked underneath. Cole reached beneath the bed, and when he climbed to his feet, he was holding Mercer in his arms, sound asleep.

"Thank you, Cole." Tears blurred her vision. She stroked her son's cheek with the backs of her fingers. "How'd you get in here?"

"Climbed the trellis, hopped onto the balcony, then entered through the window."

"You climbed that rickety old trellis?" Ren stared at him. "Do you have any idea how dangerous that was?"

"It was the quickest and easiest way to get in here," Cole said. "I did it once when I was in middle school. Your great-aunt was babysitting someone's kid and he locked himself in here."

"You're a lot taller and heavier than you were then. You could've gotten hurt," Ren pressed. Yes, she'd been terrified about Mercer being locked in here. But she'd never have forgiven herself if Cole had been seriously hurt while trying to rescue him.

"You found him!" Her mother appeared in the doorway, a hand pressed to her chest. "Where was he?"

"Under the bed, asleep," Ren whispered. "I'm going to put him to bed. I'll bathe him in the morning."

"I'm sorry, sweetheart." Her mother's face was wracked with guilt. "You probably think you can't trust me with Mercer, but—"

"It's okay, Mom. Just go back to bed." Ren squeezed her mother's hand. "It's been a long night for all of us."

"I don't know how you got in there, but we can't thank you enough." Her mother squeezed Cole's arm. "Good night, you two."

Cole carried Mercer toward his room, where he'd built a makeshift tent over Mercer's bed a few weeks ago. He laid him down.

His phone rang, signaling a video call. When he pulled the phone from his pocket, Ren could see the face of the stunning woman who was trying to reach Cole.

Cole's expression was neutral as he rejected the call.

Ren couldn't help wondering who the woman was and what her relationship with Cole was. But it was none of her business. Despite the fact that tonight might've felt dangerously close to being a date—it wasn't. She and Cole were just friends.

"Thanks for everything, Cole," Ren said. "Mercer and I enjoyed spending the day with your family."

"Does that mean you're kicking me out?" Cole asked. "Because I swiped a couple bottles of that peach brandy your mother said she likes. After the excitement of tonight, I thought we could all use a drink. Maybe watch a movie."

"You want to stay and watch a movie?" Ren ran her fingers through her hair. "That'd be nice. But if you have somewhere else to be—"

"Then I'd be there," he said.

Her heart danced and her belly fluttered. "I'll meet you downstairs as soon as I get Mercer out of these sticky clothes and into his pajamas."

Cole nodded, then left the room.

She closed her eyes, trying to slow her racing heart and remind herself that no matter what her body and heart might be feeling, she and Cole were just friends.

Fifteen

Renee tiptoed up her back steps and unlocked the door. She'd stayed at Kayleigh's wedding shower much longer than the obligatory hour or two she'd intended.

When her mother had been struck with a migraine, Cole had generously offered to babysit Mercer. Even though he and her son had become inseparable over the past few weeks, Ren hadn't wanted to impose. But Cole had convinced her that it wasn't an imposition.

Still, Cole's family had made her feel so welcome at the shower. She'd had a great time. And since Cole had insisted he and Mercer were fine when she called to check on them, she'd stayed until the party ended.

Renee went inside, toed off her shoes, then padded toward her office. The television was playing softly.

Cole was asleep on the sofa, and Mercer was tucked beneath his arm, asleep too.

The two of them were adorable. She almost hated to disturb them.

The house was still intact, and her son was in one piece. No evidence of bumps, cuts or bruises. Which was more than she could usually say on any given day. Mercer was a little daredevil with no sense of fear.

Renee lifted the arm Cole had draped over Mercer's shoulders. After carrying Mercer, already in his jammies, up to bed, she returned to her office, where Cole was still sleeping.

She muted the television and eased onto the couch beside Cole, not wanting to startle him. He looked so peaceful, but she couldn't leave Cole asleep on her sofa. He'd be much happier in his own bed.

And you'd be much happier with him in yours.

That was a horrible idea for more reasons than she was currently prepared to enumerate. Still, she was grateful to Cole. And not just for tonight. For being there whenever she'd needed him, even though the two of them were vying for the same land. Even though helping her succeed could directly impact his chances of acquiring her grandfather's property.

Ren kissed Cole's cheek. It startled him and he jumped.

He patted the space beside him in a panic. "Mercer—"

"Is fine," she assured him with a soft smile. "I put him to bed. He seems well-fed and in one piece. And so do you." She placed a gentle hand on his cheek. "Did my little guy give you any trouble?"

"None." Cole's eyes seemed to linger on her lips. "We had a great time."

"Good." Ren reluctantly dropped her hand from his face. "I brought you a plate."

"Thanks." Cole spiked a hand through his short curls. "Those little chicken nuggets Merce likes are fine. But a brother could use some adult food right about now."

She stood and extended a hand. "Need help, old man?"

"You're older than me," he reminded her.

"So we're both getting old. Do you want a hand or not?"

Cole gave her his hand. But when she tried to tug him up, he wouldn't budge, and she stumbled forward onto his lap.

"No fair." She poked his hard chest and laughed.

"*That* was for calling me old." Cole studied her with his dark, penetrating gaze.

Ren swallowed hard, her cheeks flaming with heat. She made no effort to rise from his lap, though she knew she should. Being this close to Cole, wrapped in his delicious scent with his body heat surrounding her, felt too good. She wasn't ready for this small moment between them to end.

"I had no idea you were so sensitive about your—"

Before she could finish the words, Cole cupped her cheek with his large hand and tugged her forward, his firm lips crashing into hers.

The kiss took her by surprise, but she didn't object. Instead, her eyes drifted closed and she leaned into it, enjoying the firm pressure of his lips against hers.

* * *

Cole placed a hand on Renee's back, pressing his fingertips to her soft, bare skin. He shouldn't be kissing Ren. He'd promised himself he wouldn't. Yet it had been all he could think of in the weeks since she'd first kissed him. Now that he held Ren in his arms, his lips gliding over hers, his only thought was that he wanted... *needed*...more.

Everything about this woman was profoundly sexy. The gentle sway of her hips. Her voice, as warm, sweet and soothing as honey. Her single-minded determination. Her brilliant, intricate mind. Even that damn stubborn streak he'd found himself on the wrong side of more than once. The way Ren could walk into a room, draw every man's attention and be completely oblivious to the fact.

He'd seen her sweaty and speckled with mud as she wrangled a four-year-old whose speed rivaled that of Usain Bolt. Yet all he'd been able to think of was how much he'd like to toss her over his shoulder, hop in the shower with her and lather up every inch of her gleaming brown skin.

Ren braced her hand on his shoulders, then shifted to her knees, straddling him, grinding the warm space between her luscious thighs against his growing length. Cole groaned against her lips in response, and Ren reciprocated with a breathy gasp.

Cole seized the moment, sweeping his tongue between her lips and exploring the sweet taste of her mouth. He palmed the full bottom he'd been admiring for weeks, pulling her tight against him. Intensifying the delicious sensation that made him painfully hard.

Their kiss escalated, Ren's eagerness seeming to match his ravenous desire. He ached to touch her, to taste her, to be buried deep inside her. To act on all the fantasies that had run through his mind as he'd lain in bed at night, his body aching and his brain replaying every damn word she'd uttered. Cataloging the moments that had stoked the fire in his gut and made his chest feel like it was about to explode.

Ren circled her hips, gliding up and down the ridge beneath his zipper. He swallowed her soft whimpers and matched them with his own groans, his body aching with need. He wanted to strip Ren out of that sexy little dress. Glide his hands over her soft skin. Plot the path his lips would soon take.

Cole slid the zipper down her back slowly, half expecting Ren to object. She didn't. And when he unfastened the clasps on her bra, Ren slipped the garment off as if it was an unwelcome restraint. She slid the thin straps from her shoulder, allowing the top of her dress to fall.

Cole splayed one palm on her back possessively, reveling in the sensation of her bare skin beneath his and her bare breasts smushed against his hard chest through his shirt. Ren gripped the bottom of his black Darth Vader T-shirt and tore her mouth from his just long enough to help him pull the garment over his head. She tossed it onto the floor. But when she leaned in to kiss him again, he pressed a gentle hand to her shoulder, halting her.

He sank his teeth into his lower lip as he surveyed her bare torso in the glow cast from the television. Her full breasts were perfect, the tight brown nipples standing erect, begging for his attention. He palmed one of the heavy globes, then dipped his head, capturing its beaded tip with his mouth. Cole swirled his tongue over it.

Ren shuddered, sighing softly as he licked and sucked one nipple and grazed the other with his calloused thumb. She braced her hands on his shoulders, tilted her head back and swiveled her hips.

"Fuck," he whispered against her skin. He sucked in a deep breath, trying to regain his sense of control, which Ren seemed determined to wrestle away.

Renee whimpered softly and arched her back. The sound unleashed something in him. Broke through any remaining restraint he might've had. He wanted to touch Ren. Taste her. Be buried deep inside her. As he had countless times in his imagination.

He shifted Ren onto the sofa so she was on her back, then claimed her mouth with a greedy kiss that betrayed his growing hunger for her. Ren and Mercer had become an integral part of his life these past few weeks. But the line between their friendship and whatever this was had become increasingly hazy. And now he was ready to obliterate it. To stop fighting this and let it become whatever it was.

Cole glided a hand up the soft skin of Ren's inner thigh as he continued their kiss. He cupped her sex through her lacy panties. Ren moaned softly, her legs falling open to give his hand more space. Cole slipped the damp fabric aside, gliding his fingers over her wet heat. Ren gasped, her breath coming in short, quick bursts. Her chest heaved and her whimpers grew louder as he moved his hand over her slick, hot flesh. Slowly at first. Then more quickly, matching the increasing intensity of their kiss.

"Oh!" Ren clutched his bare shoulders, her short fingernails digging into his skin when he slipped two fingers inside of her.

Yep. He'd definitely found her spot.

God, Ren was beautiful. So incredibly sensual, but in the least obvious of ways. She was his personal kryptonite now, just as she had been back then. Like she had a string wrapped around her finger that was tethered to his heart and all the messy emotions he tried so hard to avoid.

When she whimpered his name, her voice breathy and tense, it was one of the sweetest sounds he'd ever heard.

Cole kissed Ren harder as he teased her sensitive spot with his fingertips and massaged the taut bundle of nerves with his thumb.

Ren cursed and called his name, her body stiffening and her sex pulsing as he took her over the edge.

Cole nestled into the warm space between her thighs, luxuriating in Ren's warmth and the scent of her arousal. He pressed a kiss to her lips.

A slow smile lit Ren's eyes. She gripped the back of his neck, pulling him forward into another kiss, their lips crashing and their tongues tangling in a sensual dance that made him hard as steel.

Ren pushed against his shoulders, suddenly halting their kiss.

"What's wrong?" Cole's chest heaved as he studied her face. "If this is too much—"

Renee pressed a finger to his lips and cocked her head, as if listening for something.

"Ma… Ma… Ma…"

Ren sighed softly. "Cole, I'm sorry. I—"

"No need to apologize." He climbed to his feet, then pulled her up. "Go, or I can go while you…" He indicated her disheveled clothing as she tried to gather herself.

"I've got it. But could you…" Ren held up the front of her dress and turned her back to him, lifting her hair.

Cole had become an expert at removing a woman's bra with one hand. Fastening it was a totally different skill set, but he managed. "There. Good as new."

"Thanks." Ren turned around. "Did you remember to give Mercer his melatonin?"

Cole cringed as he tugged his T-shirt over his head. "I didn't. I'm sorry. We were watching TV on the couch, and I totally forgot to—"

"It's okay." Ren easily slipped back into mommy mode. "I'll give it to him now and read him a story. Hopefully, that'll do it. I'll put your plate in the microwave before I go up."

"Don't worry about it. I'll just take it back to my place."

"Oh…" Renee tucked loose strands of hair behind one ear. "Well…good night, then."

"Good night, and say good-night to Little Man for me."

"I will." Ren gave him a pained smile on her way toward the kitchen.

Cole ducked into the little bathroom tucked beneath the staircase. The steps creaked above him as Renee went up to Mercer's room. He stared at himself in the mirror as he washed his hands.

What the fuck did you just do?

Cole heaved a sigh, his heart racing. Ren was a divorced mom who was trying to build this business on her own. She was stressed-out, overwhelmed and maybe a little lonely.

Had he taken advantage of that?

Cole scrubbed a hand down his face. He'd fucked up. *Again.*

Why couldn't he ever seem to get it right where Renee was concerned?

Sixteen

Any disappointment Ren felt was allayed the moment she saw her little boy's face. When she opened his bedroom door, he sat up and grinned.

"Ma… Ma… Ma…"

"Mama missed you, too, sweetheart." She sat on the edge of Mercer's bed and hugged him tight.

Ren extended her hand and Mercer gladly swiped the fruit-flavored gummy supplement. Then he hopped down from his bed, grabbed a book of nursery rhymes and handed it to her before climbing back into bed.

Renee slipped an arm around Mercer and read him a bedtime story. Then another and another. By the end of the third story, Mercer was sound asleep again. She clicked off the light and slipped out of his room.

She went to her room and got ready for bed, putting on an old T-shirt and sleep shorts. She wrapped her hair, tied it up with her satin scarf, then put on her glasses. Ren crawled into her bed—the same bed she might've been sharing with Cole right now if Mercer hadn't awakened.

Ren sighed. Everything that had just happened between her and Cole replayed in her head. The feel of his strong hands on her skin. The taste of his mouth. The weight of his body on hers. The shudder that rippled through her when Cole had taken her over the edge.

She really needed to pull it together. She also needed to lock up after Cole.

Ren went downstairs to turn off the lights in the kitchen and nearly screamed. Cole was sitting at the table with the empty food container in front of him and a half-eaten slice of cake.

"I thought you left." Ren pressed a hand to her chest.

"I thought we should talk." Cole moved the container aside.

The hint of joy she'd felt at seeing Cole quickly faded. Cole didn't need to say the words. They were written all over his face.

This was a mistake. It can never happen again.

And maybe he was right. Trying to figure out how to navigate whatever was happening between them was a lot to ask on top of everything else going on in her life.

So she would save him the trouble.

"No need. We got caught up in the moment." Ren shrugged. "We're both adults. Stuff happens. It's forgotten."

Cole stared at her, blinking.

Is he surprised or relieved?

It didn't matter. Now that she'd said the words, he wouldn't have to. That somehow seemed better.

"Ren," Cole said, "I don't want to hurt you again." The pained look on his face seemed genuine. But still, it was another rejection.

"I'm not the lonely teenage girl desperately hoping you'll ask her to prom anymore, Cole. And I'm not looking for a relationship any more than you are." Ren stood taller.

Why did he look...*gutted*? Wasn't this the part where he breathed a sigh of relief and then got the hell out of Dodge before she could change her mind?

"I just wanted to say I'm sorry, Ren. I crossed a line I shouldn't have. I should know better than—"

"If there had been a line I hadn't wanted you to cross, I would've made that crystal clear without hesitation. What happened...it was just two consenting adults having a little fun." Ren sighed. "I know my grandfather probably asked you to watch out for us, and I appreciate everything you've done, but you are *not* responsible for me, Cole. And you don't get to dictate my choices. So stop behaving as if you're Darth Vader and you pulled me onto the dark side or something. All right?" She indicated his T-shirt.

"All right." Cole stood, picking up the empty container and discarded napkins.

"Leave it. I'll take care of this." Ren forced a smile, not wanting Cole to think she was angry. "I appreciate everything you've done tonight. Now, go home and get some sleep. You've earned it." She walked to the back door and opened it. "Good night, Cole."

"And we're still good?"

"Golden." Ren widened her painted-on smile. "Promise."

"Good night, Ren." Cole dropped a friendly kiss on her cheek. Then he stepped out onto the porch, stuffed his feet into his boots and took the path back to his own house.

Later, when Ren lay on her side in bed, her knees pulled into a fetal position, she could see the light on in Cole's bedroom through the slit in her curtains.

Was he still thinking of their kiss, too?

She doubted that Cole Abbott would lay in bed and relive their trip to third base when women who looked like supermodels kept calling his phone. Women who probably didn't have an adorable kid with a horrible sense of timing.

It was just as well. She didn't need the distraction. Mercer was her focus, and she was creating a legacy for him and for their family. Cole was the one person standing between her and her dream of resuscitating her family's farm. She needed to remember that—no matter how amazing the man's kiss was.

Ren reached under her bed and rummaged through the small container where she'd stored her great-aunt's journals and the book safe she still hadn't managed to crack. She hadn't dared to read any more since the night Cole had discovered them. She'd felt badly about invading her aunt's privacy. But there was a part of her that needed to know if her aunt's little experiment had turned out as she'd hoped it would.

She clicked on the little bedside lamp, propped her pillows against the headboard and started to read.

Cole counted aloud as he did Spider-Man push-ups, alternately drawing each knee to his elbow as he lowered himself to the floor.

He needed to focus on the effort required and the tension in his shaking muscles. On anything other than the way it had felt to hold Renee's soft, lush body against his or the sweet taste of her warm mouth.

Cole squeezed his eyes shut against the memories of that kiss that flooded his brain, even as his triceps burned and his abdominal muscles and obliques begged for mercy. He cursed, shaking his head. He'd lost count again.

No matter how many push-ups he did, he couldn't stop thinking of what had happened between them or how it had made him feel.

It had been more than *just* a kiss. And Ren had become more than just a friend.

Cole lowered himself to the floor and rolled onto his back, his chest heaving. He couldn't help glancing toward the window that faced her bedroom. The lights were out.

He draped an arm over his face and took slow, deep breaths as his heart rate slowed. On a typical Saturday night, he'd be out either in Gatlinburg or an hour away in Knoxville. But there had been nothing typical about his life in the weeks since he'd moved into Ms.

Bea's old house and become Ren and Mercer's next-door neighbor.

The two of them had slowly become a central part of his life. He couldn't make a trip past the general store or local farm supply without phoning Ren to see if she needed something. He thought of them often. Worried about them constantly. As he glanced over at the darkened house, he was deciding which floodlights to install to ensure the two of them stayed safe.

When the hell had he become that guy? The old guy who worried over everyone, imagining the worst possible scenarios and what he needed to do to protect them.

Cole got up and gathered the T-shirt and jeans he'd stripped off earlier. There was a blueberry-stained handprint on his jeans.

Mercer.

Cole had no idea how it had happened, but the kid had him wrapped around his little finger. So did his mother, for that matter. Because he'd do just about anything for either of them. Anything except walk away from his plans for the old Lockwood family farm that lay beyond their two houses. That was the only part of his plan he'd managed to stick to.

Cole liked to think of himself as a compassionate person. One who gave a hand up to struggling entrepreneurs—as Milo had once done for him. But he hadn't gotten where he was in business by being a pushover who bent over backward for the competition. And yet, with Ren, that was exactly what he was doing.

He'd lost his edge; lost his focus. He needed to finalize his plans to remodel this old house. Show Milo exactly why his proposal was the better one. And stop being so damn eager to help Ren execute her plan.

Cole turned on the shower, stripped naked and dropped his clothing into the hamper.

His phone signaled an incoming video call. And though it was late, it wasn't an unusual occurrence. He checked the name on the screen. *Lisa.* The phys ed teacher in Knoxville he'd had an off-and-on friends-with-benefits relationship with the past couple of years. A call at this time of night meant one of two things: phone sex or an invitation to spend the weekend in Knoxville for the real thing.

Cole picked up the phone, pushed the message icon and chose Currently Not Available. It was their signal indicating that they were involved with someone else.

He set the phone down and stepped into the shower.

His relationship with Ren was definitely fucking with his head and throwing him off his game, so she was already winning. Because he couldn't stop thinking of her, wishing they'd been able to finish what they'd started.

Seventeen

Renee nearly jumped out of her skin in response to Cole's distinctive knock. She hurried to the mirror by the front door and checked her hair and makeup, then fiddled with the cowl neckline and thin shoulder straps of her peachy gold satin dress.

The dress, strappy gold heels and expensive jewelry felt like a costume. She was playing the role of someone sexier and more sophisticated than she could ever hope to be.

Cole knocked again, and Ren glanced toward the back door.

She and Cole hadn't been in the same room since the night they'd scandalized her poor sofa. Cole had waved from across the way. He'd even dropped off thoughtful gifts for her and Mercer, sending a text to notify her he'd left them on the back porch. But he'd clearly been avoiding her. It was just as well. She hadn't known quite what to say to him, either.

Thanks for the finger bang, pal. But you're right. We probably shouldn't do that again. Still, I'd really, really *like to.*

But she'd committed to being Cole's plus-one at Parker and Kayleigh's wedding, so they were in for an awkward evening. Ren sucked in a deep breath, then opened the newly installed screen door with a broad smile. "Come on in. I just need to grab my purse."

"Wow." Cole's dark eyes were filled with heat as he scanned her from head to toe. He dragged a hand down his neatly trimmed beard. "You look…incredible."

"Thank you. You don't look bad yourself." Ren straightened the collar of his crisp white shirt, worn without a tie. An indigo-blue dinner jacket, belted white pants and expensive leather boots completed his look. "There. Perfect."

Cole's nostrils flared slightly as he flashed her a devilish half smile that warmed her all over. They hadn't left the house yet, and the man already had her all hot and bothered.

Ren retrieved her sparkly clutch from her office and returned to the kitchen with a flourish. "Plus-one, reporting for duty."

Cole shoved his hands in his pockets and frowned. "Ren, about the other night—"

"Unless you have something new to offer on the subject, I didn't get all fancied up tonight to be rejected again." Ren forced a smile. "Now, are we going to this wedding or what?"

"I didn't reject you, Renee, I..." Cole dragged a hand through his hair and sighed. "After you." He gestured toward the door, then he escorted her to his Jaguar F-Type, parked in her driveway.

"Nice." Ren gestured toward the sexy all-black luxury sports car. "New ride?"

"No, I keep it parked in a garage on the company lot until I can build a garage here. But I couldn't have you climbing in and out of the truck in that dress." Cole's gaze lingered on her thigh, exposed by the side split as she lowered into the passenger seat.

"Thoughtful." Ren smiled sweetly. "Now, if you could stop staring at my thigh for a moment...we have a wedding to get to. Wouldn't look good for the brother of the groom to be late."

"I was just..." Cole cleared his throat, quickly abandoning whatever excuse he was about to offer. "Right. We'd better go."

Cole got inside and pushed the black start button. The engine roared to life. After a few minutes of riding in silence, he asked, "Did Little Man get settled at your mom's all right?"

"He did." It was the first time she'd let Mercer spend the entire weekend with her mother in Knoxville. She'd video called them three times already in the twenty-four hours since she'd left him in her mother's care. "He's handling it like a champ. Me? Not so much."

Cole chuckled. "I miss the little guy."

"He misses you, too," Ren said. "But for the record, you're the one who's been avoiding me."

"I know," he admitted after a long pause. "I lost control with you that night, and I shouldn't have."

"Why not?" Ren was horrified that she'd asked. But now that it was out there, she needed an answer to the question that'd been dancing in her head for the past two weeks. "If you're not really attracted to me...fine. I get that."

"Of course, I'm attracted to you, Ren. Are you kidding me? Just look at you." He gestured toward her. "A lack of attraction isn't the issue, and it never has been."

"Then what is the issue?" She turned toward him. "Is it because of your relationship with my grandfather?"

"Not exactly."

Ren folded her arms like a pouty toddler. "Why don't you just say what you mean, Cole?"

He tightened his grip on the gear shifter. "I promised myself if I ever got a shot at fixing our friendship, I wouldn't fuck it up this time. That I'd keep things strictly platonic. I value our relationship, Ren. I don't want to hurt you again."

"Oh." Ren's chest tightened and her belly fluttered. She studied the profile of the handsome man who'd become her closest friend, despite being on opposite sides of the decision about the fate of her family's land. Despite the awkwardness of the past two weeks.

"Our friendship is important to me, too. But I'd be lying if I said I didn't think about this being *more*. Not a relationship," she clarified, in response to his panicked expression. "Neither of us is looking for that."

"You mean just sex?" Cole glanced at her quickly, then returned his attention to the road.

"I...um..." In her head, it had sounded scientific, almost clinical. She'd propose her own bad boy experiment. A basic, mutualistic relationship. Like the oxpecker and zebra or a bee and a flower. Each had something to offer that the other wanted or needed. She'd been prepared to eloquently lay out the terms. But in real time she'd been reduced to babbling like an idiot. "Yes?" *Shit.* That sounded like a question. "I mean, *yes*. Why not? Isn't that your usual MO?"

"I've had my share of no-strings relationships," Cole admitted as he entered the lot of the wedding venue and bypassed the valet stand. He parked the Jag in a space reserved for the family. Cole unbuckled his seat belt and turned toward her. "This is going to make me sound like an arrogant dick, but you insisted on honesty."

A knot tightened in her stomach. "Let's hear it."

"No-strings sex isn't hard to come by. It's the boonies. There's not a hell of a lot to do around here." Cole leaned in, as if he was about to tell her the secret of the universe. "What we have is hard to come by. At least, it has been for me. So even if I do want this..." He lifted her chin. "And make no mistake, Ren. I really, *really* want you." Cole sighed and dropped his hand from her face. "But I won't ruin a potentially lifelong friendship for a short-term fling."

"Okay." Ren reached for the door, but Cole held her arm.

He hopped out of the Jaguar and opened the door for her, escorting her toward the front entrance of the elegantly remodeled barn—another renovation project he was tremendously proud of.

"I hope you understand." Cole turned to her, just before they entered the barn door.

"I do, and I appreciate your honesty." Ren smiled sweetly. "We should remain strictly friends, and I'll find someone else to have a no-strings fling with. Shouldn't be hard. Like you said, there's not much else to do around here."

"Wait… I…you…"

Ren stood tall and posed for the photographer taking photos of arriving guests. But she was pretty sure the photo had captured Cole with his eyes wide and his bearded jaw on the floor.

"You're not serious." Cole caught up with Ren, who'd walked…no, *strutted*…her fine ass away after the photo was taken. He pulled her off to the side and whispered loud enough to be heard over the din of the small crowd and the harpist playing what he was pretty sure was a Marvin Gaye song. "You're just saying that to fuck with me, *right*?"

"Cole, you're a phenomenal friend. I adore you, and I respect your decision." Ren glanced around and lowered her voice. "But did you think because you said no I was going to lock myself in some metaphorical tower while you sleep with half the single women in the county?"

Maybe. "Of course not," he said.

She waved and flashed a smile at Jeb Dawson's son, Leonard, whom Cole had asked to fix one of Ren's tractors. The man was staring at Ren like she was barbecue chicken and he hadn't eaten in a week.

Cole's jaw clenched and his blood boiled at the thought of Len laying one of his grimy fingers on Ren.

His heart beat furiously. His neck and chest were hot. Ren was right; he was being unfair and maybe a bit sexist. But knowing that didn't make it any easier to swallow the thought of Ren being with someone else.

Cole held his hands up in surrender. "I'm sorry. It was a knee-jerk reaction. But hooking up with some random just doesn't feel like you."

"I'm here because I wanted a new start." Ren's tone softened. "Part of that new start for me is spreading my wings and trying new experiences."

"And taking risks?" Cole frowned.

"Calculated ones, like starting the farm. Yes." Ren folded her arms.

Lawd...have...mercy.

The movement accentuated the cleavage exposed by the flirty neckline of Ren's dress. It was a common gesture. One Ren made frequently. And maybe she'd done it inadvertently. But right now, it felt like she was definitely fucking with his head.

Pull it together, man.

"And you consider this bad boy experiment thing a calculated risk?"

So much for keeping cool about it.

"Yes. Now, I think we should take our seats." Ren glanced over at where Zora was gesturing for them to come and sit with her and Dallas.

Cole extended his arm and Ren took it.

They greeted Dallas and Zora—who rubbed her growing belly. Cole tweaked the chubby cheek of his niece Remi, whom Zora balanced on her lap. Seated in front of them were Max and Quinn, Sloane and the twins—Beau and Bailey—and Grandpa Joe, whose shoulder Cole squeezed. After a few minutes of chatting with his family, the harpist started to play "Lovin' You" by Minnie Ripperton. Cole glanced up to see Parker escorting their mother down the aisle in a floor-length mauve dress. There was an effervescent grin on her face. Iris Abbott was on cloud nine, watching another one of her children walk down the aisle.

Parker kissed their mother's cheek and joined their brother Blake and cousin Benji, who were already standing up front.

Parker's placid expression revealed only a hint of his underlying terror. There was a good chance his brother would either lose his lunch or bolt like a rabbit.

Next, his sister-in-law Savannah floated down the aisle in a beige one-shoulder gown, followed by Kayleigh's sister, Evelisse.

Evvy's eyes filled with unshed tears as she carried both her bouquet and a framed photograph of her and Kayleigh's parents, who'd passed years earlier.

Next came his nephew, Davis, in his little beige suit—to match that of the groom and his groomsmen—and a tiny bow tie. In one hand, he held a small satin pillow with both rings. In the other, he held a leash wrapped with vines and flowers. On the other end of the leash was Kayleigh's golden retriever, Cricket: the flower dog. She tugged Davis down the aisle, garnering chuckles from the crowd.

The harpist shifted to another song Cole recognized: "A Thousand Years," by Christina Perri. Everyone turned toward the back, where Kayleigh stood looking ethereal in a bohemian, all-lace wedding gown. Her wild red curls were crowned with a jeweled vine halo sparkling with pale pink crystals and pearls.

Kayleigh clutched Duke's arm. He patted her hand reassuringly and whispered something to her. The bride nodded and seemed to relax. Kayleigh broadened her smile, her eyes focused on her husband-to-be standing at the head of the aisle.

His typically stoic brother's eyes were filled with emotion as he eagerly awaited his bride.

Duke kissed Kayleigh's cheek, then handed her off to Parker before taking his seat beside their mother.

Parker looked nervous as he extended his arm to Kayleigh, whispering loudly that she looked beautiful.

The expression on his brother's face could only be described as…*love*.

For the first time in his memory, Cole truly envied Parker.

The ceremony was simple but beautiful. When the couple was declared husband and wife, the barn erupted with applause.

Afterward, when the crowd began mingling, Cole's mother, who was still beaming, slipped her arm through his and whispered, "And then there was one."

She glanced over at Renee, who held Remi as she chatted with Quinn. His mother's smile widened. "But maybe not for long."

* * *

A few hours later, Cole stood at the old wooden bar with his brothers and cousin Benji. They'd had dinner, the toasts and the couple's first dance. Now he sipped his beer, oblivious to their conversation as he scanned the crowd.

"Looking for Renee again?" Blake sipped his bourbon, barely able to contain an amused grin.

"You know he is," Max said, chuckling. "For you two not to be involved, you're doing a convincing imitation of a jealous lover, Cole."

Cole turned up the bottle and drained it. Prompted by his friendship with Quinn and his promise to Zora, he and Max had hashed things out and *finally* called a truce. So calling Max a meddling dickhead, while accurate, wouldn't be conducive to their new brotherly vibe.

"Leave Cole alone. Maybe he's just not ready to admit that he wants to be more than friends with Renee." Parker looked happy but mentally exhausted.

The day had required a lot of face time for Parker, who was admittedly far better at non-peopley things: like spreadsheets and data.

"Another beer for me and another old-fashioned for my wise older brother," Cole called to the bartender before turning to his brothers again. He lowered his voice. "So maybe I am into her. But I want the best for Ren and Mercer. And we all know I'm not it."

"That's bullshit," Max said. "You're making excuses because you're scared of commitment."

Cole clenched his jaw, hating that his brothers could see right through him.

"Commitment can be intimidating," Blake said quickly. "But I think we'd all agree that what we've gained is well worth any sacrifices we had to make."

Parker, Max and Benji all nodded in agreement.

"I'm glad you guys are so happy. I'm happy for you," Cole said. "But marriage isn't for everyone."

"True, and we all probably felt that way at some point. But when the right woman comes along...everything feels *different*." Parker nodded toward the dance floor, where Kayleigh was dancing with Grandpa Joe to Nat King Cole's "L-O-V-E"—a favorite song of their grandfather's.

A few feet away, his parents swayed together on the floor and Savannah danced with Davis.

"You had a thing for Renee back in high school, right?" Max asked. He didn't wait for an answer. "Then this is a second chance for you two. Take it from me, bruh. If you're as into her as it seems, you do *not* want to throw away a second shot."

"What if neither of us is looking for anything serious?" Cole asked, his gaze landing on Renee, who was chatting with Zora and Dallas.

Blake, Parker, Benji and Max all broke out into raucous laughter.

"I'm pretty sure that's what we all told ourselves in the beginning," Blake finally said.

"But if that's truly the case, neither of you have anything to lose." Parker sipped his old-fashioned.

Cole shifted his gaze to where Len approached Renee and asked her to dance—for the second time that night. He gripped his beer bottle tightly, his jaw clenched.

Maybe Parker was right. He and Renee were sensible adults. They could certainly navigate sex while keeping their friendship intact, couldn't they?

Or maybe he was just setting himself up for a fall.

"Thank you for a lovely evening, Cole. The wedding was beautiful. I'm glad I was there for it." Renee turned to Cole after he'd insisted on walking her to her door.

"It was a pretty amazing day." Cole rubbed his chin absently, seemingly distracted.

"Good night." Ren turned to go inside.

"Wait, Ren." Cole grasped her hand. "This…no-strings thing you want… I'll do it."

Renee spun around and stared at Cole, her heart beating faster. This was what she'd wanted, wasn't it? So why did she suddenly feel like she was in the midst of a panic attack?

"I thought you were worried it would ruin our friendship," she stammered.

"I am, but no matter how much I try to convince myself this is a bad idea… I can't stop thinking of you, Ren, and wanting you."

"Are you sure that—"

He cradled her face in his hands, and captured her mouth in a kiss that made her heart beat double time and filled her body with heat.

Cole glided his tongue between her lips, which eagerly parted. He dropped his large hands to her waist and pinned her between his muscled body and the wall behind her, his hardened length pressed to her belly. He kissed Ren until her legs were weak and the space between her thighs pulsed and ached. Until the intense beating of her heart rumbled through her chest like peals of thunder in a good old-fashioned Southern storm.

Finally, he pulled his mouth from hers, leaving her breathless and wanting. Desperate for the heat of his body. Cole propped a hand on the wall above her, his chest rising and falling, his face a few inches from hers.

"You still think I'm not sure?" Cole's voice was raw and husky as his lips brushed the outer shell of her ear. "Or is that the kiss of a man who's been dreaming about all of the ways I can make you scream my name?"

Ren swallowed hard, her hands trembling as she recalled that night on the sofa in her office. Even the memory of that night made her body react.

After all this time, Cole Abbott still had the ability to leave her babbling and tongue-tied. But here he was, offering exactly what she'd wanted…even before she'd been inspired by her aunt's journals to conduct a bad boy experiment of her own.

"Why don't you think about it and get back to me?" Cole's eyes glinted and that sexy mouth of his pulled to one side in an impish smirk.

"That won't be necessary." Ren swallowed hard, her head light and her chest heaving after the dreamy kiss that had left her breathless. "Your place in an hour?"

Cole's dark eyes glimmered, and his nostrils flared. "Hydrate, sweetheart." He winked. "It's gonna be one hell of a night."

Eighteen

An hour after Cole had kissed her senseless on her back porch, Renee made the trek between her house and his, the gravel path crunching beneath her feet. It was a short distance. But every single step required all her effort.

Ren was terrified and thrilled and completely unsure about this. But she'd been thinking about it for the past two months, inspired by her aunt's bold proposal more than fifty years ago. And by her mother's fear that she would never experience that one great affair that curled her toes and left her with a lifetime of fond memories.

Ren wanted that.

She'd spent her entire life being the good girl. Doing all the things she was *supposed* to do. What she'd been left with was a decade of faked orgasms and a broken marriage. Nothing close to the experience her great-aunt had written about.

Despite what she'd said to Cole earlier, Renee couldn't possibly imagine doing this with someone she didn't know and trust. And despite her initial misgivings, which had proved wrong, she did trust Cole. She'd entrusted him with her son—the most precious thing in the world to her. She could trust him with this, too.

Ren climbed the stairs to Cole's back porch. She lifted a quivering hand and knocked on the newly installed screen door, which matched her own. The lights were on inside and there was music playing, but there was no answer. Ren knocked again.

Still no answer.

Evidently, the universe was trying to prevent her from making a colossal mistake. Or maybe Cole had changed his mind. Either way, she should heed the warning and walk away now. Pretend none of this had ever happened.

Renee turned and started down the stairs. Suddenly, the door swung open, taking her by surprise. She missed a step, tripping but catching herself on the banister before she face-planted in the gravel.

Graceful, Renee. You're a regular Misty Copeland.

"Ren?" Cole hurried down the stairs. "Are you okay?"

"Yeah, I'm fine. I thought maybe you'd… I don't know." She shrugged. "Changed your mind."

She was flustered and rambling like a fool. Yep, this was definitely a bad idea.

Stop talking and make a graceful exit, if that's even possible at this point.

"Not a chance, sweetheart." Cole extended a hand. "C'mon inside."

Renee swallowed hard, her hand trembling as she placed it inside his.

Don't chicken out now.

Cole led her into the kitchen. Like hers, it was outdated. It reminded her of her Aunt Bea standing at the old stove making fried corn or her famous chicken and dumplings—the first thing Ren had ever learned to cook.

"Still feels weird being here, huh?" Cole's voice shook her from her temporary daze.

"Very."

They entered the living room where an exercise mat and weights were on the floor.

"You were working out. I'm sorry. I shouldn't have disturbed you." Ren glanced at the equipment. "I know it's really late and—"

"Renee..." Cole drew her closer, pulling her attention back to him. His gaze was soft and warm as he stroked her cheek. "It's okay. We both know why you came here." He managed to say the words without sounding cocky. "But I need to hear it from you. Tell me exactly what you want from me."

Ren's head was spinning. No one had ever asked her that. Not in a relationship or her career. And now that he had, she wasn't quite sure what to say.

So instead, she clutched Cole's white Abbott Construction & Development T-shirt, pulled him closer and pressed her lips to his. Cole splayed one large hand on her back. The other arm snaked around her waist, tugging her lower body tight against his.

He kissed her as if he was a starving man, and she was the only sustenance he'd ever need.

This was why she'd come here.

She needed to get over her fear. Be clear about what she wanted, as she'd learned to do working in labs filled with men who didn't think she could possibly have the answers.

Ren slid a trembling hand down Cole's chest and over his taut abs. She cupped him as they continued their heated kiss, then glided her hand up and down his length through the thin fabric of his basketball shorts. She was delighted by Cole's tortured groan in response to her touch. He intensified their kiss, his tongue searching hers and his strong hands gripping her bottom.

His eager response emboldened her. She glided her fingertips beneath the waistband of his shorts and wrapped her fingers around the width of his heated flesh. She spread the silky drops of fluid at its tip with her thumb.

Ren swallowed Cole's soft gasp. Felt his back stiffen beneath her fingertips. She closed her fist around the velvety skin, pumping him slowly at first, then harder and faster.

Cole broke their kiss, lightly grasping her wrist. His chest heaved as he gently tugged her hand from his shorts. He stared at her, his dark eyes filled with need.

"Ren, I'm trying to be good here. But I swear, baby girl, you are fucking killing me right now," Cole whispered roughly, his breathing heavy. "I need you to say the words."

"If you already know why I'm here, why do I need to say it?" She shrugged innocently.

Ren tugged her hand from his grip and slowly slid down the zipper of her short denim dress. She shrugged off the dress, revealing a sheer bra and panties with strategic bits of lace.

Cole's eyes widened, and his Adam's apple bobbed when he swallowed.

"You look…*incredible*," Cole stammered. He took her hand. "But I still need you to be clear about what you want."

"I'd think this is pretty clear." Ren gestured toward her barely clad body. "Do you really need more than that?"

"Yes," he said emphatically. "We need to be clear about what this is, Ren. If you're really looking for a friends-with-benefits situation, I'm your man. But if you're looking for more…" Cole rubbed the back of his neck. "I can't give you that."

"You think I'm shopping for a husband and a father for my son?" Ren pulled her hand from his and folded her arms over her chest.

"Not consciously." Cole shoved his hands in his pockets, which made his hard-on more evident. "But the stakes are higher for you. You have your future and Mercer's to think about."

"Mercer is my life, and I'd do anything for him. But I can take care of us. I don't need you for that. Tonight is about what *I* want. And what I want is simple, Cole. Sex with no strings, no commitments and no expectations."

"Come here." Cole's voice was gruff. His dark eyes were filled with heat. When she stepped closer, he looped his arms around her waist.

Renee shuddered at the feel of him pressed to her belly.

"I'm no fairy-tale prince, Ren. I'm not sweet or gentle. And I'm no one's knight in shining armor. I'm not the man you deserve."

"But you're the man I want." Renee shivered beneath his intense stare as she lightly gripped his strong biceps.

She was nervous and quivering. Maybe even a little nauseous. She'd never done anything like this before. But she was sure—*damn sure*—she wanted this. That she wanted him.

Ren pressed a kiss to his chest. Then another to his shoulder. Then another to his neck.

Cole hauled her closer and captured her mouth in a greedy, demanding kiss. His fingers bit into the flesh exposed by the barely-there panties as he gripped her bottom. She'd probably have bruises in the shape of his handprints tomorrow. But it would be worth it. The sensation, which danced along the razor's edge between pleasure and pain, stoked the growing heat between her thighs and made her wet for him. Her already sensitive nipples grew taut as they brushed against his rock-hard chest.

Cole was leaving a mark on her skin and staking his claim on her body. Something deep inside her chest reveled at the thought of being claimed by this man whom she'd come to adore in so many ways. This was why she'd come here: a bad boy experiment of her own. One she'd never forget.

Cole stood in his bedroom staring at Ren, his chest heaving and his pulse racing.

He stripped off his T-shirt and tossed it to the floor, loving the feel of Renee's bare skin against his as he resumed their heated kiss. Cole had one clear thought in his head. He needed Ren in his bed this instant. But behind that thought was a much fuzzier one.

What will happen to our friendship after this?

Cole pushed the question aside, determined to focus on the hunger in Ren's kiss, the sweet taste of her warm mouth and the sensation of her soft curves cradled against him.

He'd often imagined this moment as a high school senior. It was a fantasy that had infiltrated his brain again when Renee had returned to Magnolia Lake. He was eager to make up for lost time.

His hands explored Ren's lush curves. His body ached with his need for this incredible woman. But his chest expanded with the feelings he had for Renee.

It's just sex. Don't be weird about it.

Only, it didn't feel like just sex. Because it was Ren.

Cole lifted her onto the bed; the covers were already pulled back. He trailed kisses along Ren's neck and shoulder, then pulled down the front of the sheer bra so the fabric framed her perfect breasts—round and firm. Her taut nipples, hidden by small patches of lace, had teased him from the moment Ren had stripped out of that minidress.

He dipped his head, covering one beaded tip with his mouth, loving the way Ren arched her back in response. Cole teased and sucked her hardened nipple as Ren squirmed and whimpered. Her dewy, freshly showered skin tasted sweet, like the pomegranate-scented body wash she used.

Cole kissed his way down her belly and over the sheer fabric. He roughly pulled aside the panel of fabric that shielded her sex. Inhaled the dizzying scent of her arousal as he studied her glistening pink flesh. Cole's eyes drifted shut as he swiped his tongue over her engorged flesh.

Ren shuddered and gasped. Cole couldn't help smiling up at her. She was so wet for him, her body so responsive. Just one taste of her salty but sweet essence and he was addicted.

He shifted the fabric further, resisting the urge to tear it. Then he licked and sucked, teasing her with his tongue and his fingers, taking Ren higher and higher.

She dug her heels into the mattress and tangled her fingers in his short curls, her touch tentative.

Cole glanced up at Ren, who seemed embarrassed that he'd caught her watching him as he tongued her. A deep smile spread across his face.

"Show me *exactly* where you want my mouth," he said between kisses to her slick flesh.

"Wh-what?" she stammered. "I don't want to—"

"Do it. *Now.*"

Ren gently repositioned his head. When his tongue ran over her clit, she gasped, then her eyes drifted closed.

"I need to see those beautiful brown eyes." Cole glided his tongue over her firm clit, and she shuddered. "I want you to watch me taste every last drop."

Ren's eyes widened and she swallowed hard. But she kept her eyes open, as he'd demanded. She swiveled her hips and rode his tongue like she was the registered owner who held the title and keys to it. Like he belonged to her.

As she guided his head, her touch was tentative at first. But as he took her higher, she directed his head more deliberately, grinding her sex against his eager mouth.

Finally, her legs shook, and her muscles tensed, her head lolling backward as she called his name again and again.

Cole pressed feathery kisses to her quivering flesh. Trailed them up her inner thigh, over her belly and between the valley of her full breasts as her chest rose and fell.

He was hard as steel, aching to finally be inside her. Cole climbed off the bed and stripped naked.

Ren's gaze dropped to his painfully hard shaft. She watched the sway of it as he moved about the room. He retrieved the box of condoms he'd yet to unpack since his move and grabbed a strip of them. He ripped one packet off and opened it, dropping the rest on the small table beside his bed.

"Bra and panties off," he practically growled as he rolled the condom on.

Ren complied without complaint, and he crawled beneath the covers, hovering over her. He kissed Ren's shoulder, then her neck, before kissing her lush lips again.

Cole wrapped his arms around Ren as he kissed her, then grabbed his length, pumping it before he pressed it to her slick entrance. He slowly glided inside her wet heat, allowing her body to adjust to his width while they continued their passionate kiss. When he was fully seated, he cursed beneath his breath, an involuntary groan of pleasure escaping his mouth.

Being with Ren, filling her with every inch of him, felt incredible. Sent an intense wave of pleasure rolling up his spine.

Cole planted a hand on either side of Ren as he slowly rocked his hips. His gaze was locked with hers as he moved inside her, his pelvis grinding against her clit. He watched as Ren's pleasure spiraled, their movements bringing them both closer to the edge.

Ren moaned softly. She clenched his biceps, her fingernails digging into his skin as she cried out again. Her sex pulsed around his heated flesh, until finally he too had tumbled over the edge, his body stiffening as he arched his back, cursing and calling her name.

Cole dropped to the mattress beside Renee. He wrapped her in his arms, pulling her to him. Then he kissed her damp forehead, both of them trying to catch their breath. Ren pressed her cheek to his chest, then lifted her head and smiled. She pressed a soft kiss to his mouth. "That was amazing."

Cole cradled Ren's cheek and kissed her again. "Yes, it was."

What was it about Ren that made everything feel… new and different? More consequential?

Cole remembered what Parker had said earlier that night.

When the right woman comes along...everything feels different.

He pushed his brother's words out of his head, then kissed her again before going to the bathroom. When he'd returned, Ren had drifted off to sleep.

His mouth curved in a soft smile.

So much for round two.

He turned off the light, slipped under the covers and cradled Ren's naked body against his. But he couldn't fall asleep. Parker's words kept filtering through his brain.

They'd spent one night together. So why did it feel like he was already addicted to Renee? Instinctively, he knew one time with her would never be enough.

Nineteen

Ren awoke wrapped in the warmth of Cole's embrace as he snored softly, both of them naked.

She was pretty sure it was a violation of the friends-with-benefits code to fall asleep in said friend's bed. And a general rookie mistake to fall asleep with her contact lenses still in.

Ren blinked repeatedly, trying to loosen the lenses, which had cemented themselves to her eyeballs over the course of the night. Her vision was blurry and sensitive to the light spilling into the room.

She needed to get dressed and get back home. Preferably before Cole woke up.

Renee carefully lifted Cole's heavy arm and slipped from beneath it, falling onto the floor in the process.

Luckily, she caught her balance, bracing her hands on the floor.

"Not a good look, Renee. Especially naked," Ren whispered to herself as she stood up straight.

"I kind of liked it." Cole's gravelly morning voice startled her. He grinned. "You didn't quite stick the landing, but the part where your ass was in the air was spectacular."

Ren snatched the duvet up over her body, shielding her essential parts. Only the thin sheet was left on the bed, making Cole's early morning erection rather apparent.

"I…um…good morning?" Ren glanced around the room for something else to cover herself with.

"T-shirts are in those two bottom drawers." Cole indicated his dresser. "Take whatever you want."

Ren dropped the cover and ducked over to the dresser. She fished out a shirt with Cookie Monster on it that read 'Bout That Street Life and put it on. She couldn't help laughing, and it alleviated some of the awkwardness.

"Good choice." Cole shrugged on his boxer briefs and yawned. "Breakfast?"

"No, thank you. I should go." She slipped on her underwear, which she found kicked beneath the bed.

"Why?" Cole asked.

"Because I shouldn't have spent the night here."

"Why not?" He sank onto the bed and yawned again.

"Because you didn't invite me to." Ren slipped her arms out of the T-shirt long enough to put her bra on underneath it. "And since I've never seen a woman leave your place during the day, I'm assuming they don't usually spend the night."

"You've been staking out the house every morning?" Cole rubbed his neck.

"No, of course not." Ren's face went hot. "But I can see your house and driveway from my bedroom." She slipped her arms back through the sleeves. "I figured if there was no car in your drive and you didn't take anyone home the next day on your way to work—"

"Maybe we need to clarify the meaning of the words *staking out my house*." Cole chuckled dryly. He stood, rubbing one eye as he lumbered in her direction, clearly still half-asleep. "And you're right, I don't normally have overnight guests. But with us, it just kind of felt natural." He shrugged.

"Also, I fell asleep before you could send me home." Ren smirked.

"There's that, too." Cole held up a finger, then laughed when she rolled her eyes. "I'm kidding. Seriously, I'm glad you stayed." He slipped his arms around her waist and nuzzled her neck. "Otherwise, I'd have to eat breakfast all alone, and I wouldn't have a shower buddy." Cole grinned.

"You want to shower…*together*?"

"You're the one starting an eco-friendly farm. And you did say conserving water was high on the priority list," he hedged. His erection pressed against her back as he tightened his arms around her.

She should really say no. But taking a shower together sounded…nice. And wasn't the point of the bad boy experiment to try new things?

"Okay, yes to the shower. But I've been thinking..." Ren slipped out of his arms, turning to face him.

"All right." Cole folded his arms, his legs spread wide. "What is it?"

God, this man is handsome. Even when half-dressed and at half-mast.

"Last night was amazing, and I'd really like to do this again."

Cole's mouth curved in a half smile. "I'm one hundred percent with you on that."

"Good." The tension in Ren's shoulders eased a bit. "But this can only happen when Mercer is away."

"Agreed." He studied her face, one eyebrow shifting upward. "There's something else."

It hadn't been a question.

"I'd like to keep this between us."

"Whatever you want, sweetheart," Cole agreed. "But my entire family already thinks there's something happening between us. We're fighting an uphill battle on that one."

Ren nodded and sighed. She'd figured as much. "Okay. Still, I'd really rather my grandparents not know that we're—"

"Fuck buddies?" One of his thick eyebrows lifted as he rubbed his beard.

"I prefer Friends U Can Keep," she said.

"Good song." Cole smirked. "Deal. Now, I have a request."

"Let me guess... No spending the night?" Ren asked.

"You can spend the night anytime you'd like." Cole tugged her closer by his T-shirt, then looped his arms around her waist as she gazed up at him. "But this can't make things weird between us. This friendship is too important to me."

Ren smiled, her eyes pricking and her heart expanding with affection. She nodded. "Promise."

"Then we're good." Cole wrapped Ren in a hug that lifted her off her feet.

She squealed with surprise and smacked his hard abs playfully once he'd set her down. "I need to brush my teeth and do something with my hair."

Cole squatted beside one of the moving boxes along the wall and rummaged inside. He produced a sealed box and handed it to her. "That's the extra head that came with my electric toothbrush."

"Thank you." She held the box to her chest. "Got a comb in that box?"

"I'm kind of digging the raised-by-wolves look," Cole teased. "But there is one more thing… I thought maybe you'd like to come to brunch at my parents' house this afternoon. It's a send-off for Parker and Kayleigh before their honeymoon on her friend's island in the Caribbean."

"Isn't this kind of a family thing?" A knot tightened in her stomach.

"You and Merce have kind of become family." Cole shrugged nonchalantly.

Ren's brain was screaming that it was a mistake. But she liked being with Cole and his family. The trick was not to make more out of this than it was. They were friends, and she'd be hanging out with her friend's family. Nothing unusual about that.

"Then thank you, I'd love to come."

Cole's eyes darkened and he sank his teeth into his lower lip. He tugged her forward, slipping his arms around her waist.

"Say that again." His voice was a husky whisper.

"Thank you?"

He shook his head and licked his lower lip. "The other part."

"I'd love to come?" She looked at him quizzically.

A devilish grin spanned the width of his handsome face. "And I'd love to make you come…again and again and again."

"Ahh…" Her nipples tightened and the space between her thighs pulsed at the prospect of a repeat performance. "I'd really, *really* like that, too."

Twenty

Ren hummed to herself as she stood in the full-length mirror of her hotel room and pulled her dress up over her hips. She and Cole had grown close in the months since they'd become neighbors. But the feelings of friendship and affection had grown exponentially in the weeks since she and Cole had become lovers, too. Now, she was preparing for her second Abbott wedding in just three weeks.

Max and Quinn were getting married at Bazemore Orchards, owned by Quinn's grandfather, Dixon Bazemore. And by a twist of fate, Ren got to be a part of their love story.

Quinn's best friend from college was supposed to be her matron of honor, but Naomi had gotten into an accident and was unable to attend the wedding. By the end of Parker and Kayleigh's honeymoon send-off brunch, Quinn and Zora had hatched a plan for Zora to replace Naomi as the matron of honor while Ren took Zora's place as a bridesmaid, who would be coupled with Cole as groomsman.

Renee declined at first. Mainly because she assumed it would be weird for Cole. But when he'd reminded her that she was his date for the night anyway and suggested it would be fun. She couldn't say no with the entire Abbott family imploring her to say yes.

At first, she felt as if she was crashing the intimate prewedding festivities. But after spending the past two days at a luxury boutique hotel in downtown Knoxville eating, primping and celebrating the impending nuptials with Quinn, her family and the Abbotts, Renee felt more at ease. They clearly wanted her there, and she felt as if she belonged. Something she hadn't ever really felt at her ex's family events.

Ren slipped the one-shoulder, floor-length, peach-colored gown up over her strapless bra and reached behind her to zip it.

"Let me get that, beautiful." Cole entered through the connected door between their hotel rooms. He zipped the back of her dress, then looped his arms around her waist from behind. His beard scraped her skin when he dropped a kiss on her bare shoulder. As he slowly kissed his way up her neck, her nipples beaded, and she could feel him growing hard against her back. "You look…stunning."

Ren wriggled out of Cole's grasp.

"Oh no, you don't." Ren smoothed down her dress.

"You are *not* wrinkling this dress or messing up the expensive hair and makeup your future sister-in-law's family sprung for. Besides, we need to be downstairs for the limo bus in twenty minutes. And we have to be on time, so your brother won't see Quinn when she and her parents take their limo to the venue."

"Right." Cole shoved a hand in his pocket. "Knowing my sister, she'll be calling us if we aren't downstairs in ten minutes. She's taking her promotion to matron-of-honor *very* seriously."

"She is, but it's kind of adorable." Renee smiled. "Quinn and Zora have become good friends. Zora just wants to make sure Max and Quinn's day is perfect. Can you blame her?"

"No, I guess not." Cole straightened his peach-colored tie and smoothed down the collar of his white shirt. Both colors looked fresh and crisp against his blue groomsman suit.

Cole seemed to get a little more handsome every day. More so in the weeks since they'd been together. Or maybe it was just her perception of him that continued to deepen as they had lain in bed at night sharing their lives and catching up on each other's pasts.

"Perfect. Ready to go?" She smoothed down her high topknot, then picked up the little sequined purse with her lipstick and cell phone.

"I'll go back through my room and meet you downstairs, like last night." Cole inched toward the door to his room.

Ren grabbed his wrist and tugged him forward. She smiled broadly, her heart full.

"That isn't necessary. I'm not saying we advertise that you spent last night in my bed. But since Quinn requested that we have adjoining rooms away from all the other guests… I have the feeling that particular cat is out of the bag and strutting down Main Street by now."

Cole laughed. He threaded his fingers through hers and dropped a kiss on her temple. "Let's go."

Cole took his place on one side of the wedding arbor constructed of long, thin, entwined branches and decorated with sheer white panels of fabric, greenery and the most beautiful array of flowers in white, peach and orange.

He was standing farthest away from the groom. Parker, Quinn's youngest brother, Marcus, Blake and Dallas filled in the spaces between them. Dixon escorted Quinn's mother to her seat. Then Cole's parents made their way down the aisle to their seats. The music started and everyone looked up the aisle where Renee stood in her peach gown. She was gorgeous, but he could sense the sheer terror she seemed to feel.

Cole gave her a broad smile and placed a hand over his heart, signaling that she took his breath away. Ren's smile deepened and she stood taller. Her chin tipped upward as she moved down the aisle toward him.

Ren gave him a grateful smile, then took her place at the opposite end of the other side of the arbor.

Once the rest of the bridal party filed in, the music switched to Pachelbel's "Canon in D."

The bride looked beautiful in her off-white lace gown as she clutched her father's arm. They moved slowly down the white runner strewn with peach-and-orange flower petals. Her hair was up and twisted in a vine of peach, white and orange flowers.

Quinn's father kissed her cheek and handed her off to Max, who was overcome with emotion at the sight of his bride. Max took Quinn's hand, mouthing the words, *You look incredible*, as he escorted her beneath the arbor to join the officiant.

Cole was surprisingly touched by the scene. He was truly happy for his brother and Quinn. Despite his differences with Max, he was glad that he and Quinn had found their way back to each other and were starting a new life together.

During the ceremony, Quinn read the poem "In and Out of Time" by Maya Angelou, which she said was a favorite of Max's. The final verse was tattooed in script on her back, visible through the sheer back of her dress.

Then Max told the story of his own tattoo: Quinn's initials and lines from her favorite poem by Robert Frost. He read the poem, "Stopping by Woods on a Snowy Evening" and explained that it reminded Quinn of one of her favorite memories of her grandmother, whose wedding ring was now part of Quinn's engagement ring.

Cole honestly hadn't given much thought to the weddings he'd attended. He'd only cared about how everyone had looked and whether the food was good, the alcohol was flowing, and the music kept him on the dance floor. But he'd been moved by Parker's wedding a few weeks ago and by Max and Quinn's highly emotional ceremony.

By the time Max and Quinn had been declared man and wife, there were few dry eyes in the house. Cole glanced over at Renee. Quinn was a beautiful bride. But though it was his new sister-in-law's day, Renee was the only woman in the room he had eyes for. When her gaze met his, she smiled at him and gave him a discreet wave.

His heart clenched and it felt harder to breathe. It wasn't a feeling Cole was accustomed to. One that nearly knocked him off his feet.

Was he falling for Renee? And did she feel the same?

Twenty-One

Renee dried her hair after her shower with Cole. The reception had gone on late into the night and they were getting ready for bed. She wore a borrowed T-shirt of his that said, “I’m not weird, I’m limited edition,” and a pair of lacy bikini panties.

Cole returned to the room with a fresh bucket of ice. He set the bottle of peach brandy Quinn and Max had gifted the members of the wedding party in the bucket and agitated it between his palms. Then he slipped his arms around her waist and kissed her.

“I’m glad you’re here. I wouldn’t have wanted to do this with anyone else.” Cole cupped her cheek. A soft smile turned up the edges of his mouth.

Renee gazed into Cole’s dark eyes. Her heart swelled with all the things she felt for this handsome, generous, sweet man she'd come to care for and rely on so much these past few months.

It was something she couldn't have imagined when she'd first encountered Cole again at the general store. But now…it was heartbreaking to imagine her and Mercer's life without Cole in it.

Her son loved Cole. It was written all over Mercer's little face. And she understood exactly how her son felt. Because her own heart was bursting with her growing love and admiration for Cole.

Their relationship was a complicated dance. Friends. Next-door neighbors. Competitors. *Lovers.*

Growing up, Renee had become exceptionally good at compartmentalizing her feelings, something she'd watched her parents—who were both military officers—do. She'd convinced herself she could handle her unconventional relationship with Cole with the same logical approach. That she could simply enjoy their tryst and growing friendship with the same detachment.

That ship had sailed, because she was in deep. Sucked into a swirling tsunami of emotions that tugged her deeper still.

"Baby, what's wrong?" Cole brushed her cheek with his calloused thumb.

Renee struggled to hold back the unshed tears that made his handsome face a blur. "Make love to me, Cole. Like I'm yours. Like this thing we have is real."

His eyes widened momentarily as he studied her face. Cole's pained expression reminded her that she wasn't his. That she never would be.

Ren's forehead and cheeks stung with embarrassment. She pulled away from him, but Cole pinned her in place.

His only response was a slow, sweet kiss. The taste of his mouth was a mélange of smooth, rich King's Finest bourbon, tart apple crumb pie and sweet vanilla ice cream. Her body instantly reacted.

And that was what she needed to focus on. The physicality of their coupling. The passion Cole ignited in her. A feeling she'd thought herself incapable of during seven long years of marriage in which faked orgasms were the norm and her desire for the man she shared a bed with had waned through the years.

She'd begun to wonder if Dennis was right. That she was cold and clinical. Incapable of this sort of fiery passion. Evidently, they'd both been wrong. Because Cole had stirred those feelings in her and so much more. Made her see herself in an entirely new light.

Cole hadn't changed her. He'd simply provided a space where she was comfortable being herself. Discovering what she liked in bed and out. She couldn't thank him enough for that.

But as he swept her in his arms and carried her to his bed, Ren tried to quiet the growing chorus of voices in her brain that whispered *Why can't this be real?*

She'd fallen hard for Cole, despite their agreement to keep things casual. Despite his insistence he wasn't interested in a serious relationship.

Cole obviously didn't feel the same, so she needed to pull it together. Compartmentalize. Enjoy this bad boy experiment for what it was and not ruin the moment.

He laid her in his bed and stripped off the shorts he'd

been wearing commando. Cole opened the side table drawer and sheathed himself, then stalked toward her.

She slipped his borrowed T-shirt over her head and wiggled out of her underwear, tossing both onto the pile of clothing on the floor.

Cole climbed into bed and kissed her again. He kissed down her neck and shoulders. Over her breasts, teasing the hardened tips. He trailed slow, deliberate kisses down her belly. Finally, he gazed up at her with a glint in his dark eyes. He spread her with his thumbs and tasted her.

Renee shuddered as much from the intense pleasure that rippled up her spine as from the anticipation of the next stroke of his skilled tongue. Cole took another swipe at her engorged flesh, then another. She writhed, her hips squirming as she gripped the sheets.

She shut her eyes, lost in the delicious sensations, as she tried not to scream his name at the top of her lungs.

Cole stopped, and Ren opened her eyes.

"You know I love it when you watch me." Cole's voice was low and husky. "I love seeing your reaction to every single stroke." He swiped his tongue over her slick flesh, and she trembled.

She liked watching him, too. More than she would've ever imagined.

"Don't ever hold back with me, Ren," Cole whispered between lazy licks of her flesh. His cool breath ghosted over her heated skin. "Whatever you want, whatever you need...*that's* why I'm here, sweetheart. I want to give you everything you've ever desired. Everything you've been afraid to ask for."

Renee's eyes stung with tears. But she couldn't form the words. Couldn't tell him how much she wanted him. How much she needed him in her and her son's life. That she'd been happier these past few months than she'd ever been before. The joy she felt waking up with Cole's arms wrapped around her, clutching her to him as if she were his security blanket.

She was terrified of losing all of that once their little experiment ended.

Because Cole *would* eventually walk away. He'd assured her of that from the very beginning. Warned her that she shouldn't get too attached. And she'd run full steam through both of those warnings and opened her heart to him. But it honestly hadn't felt like a choice. She'd fallen for Cole *despite* her determination not to.

Cole slipped two fingers inside her, teasing that hidden place that sent her hurtling toward the clouds, as he intensified the speed and pressure of his tongue.

Ren cursed, her heels digging into the mattress as she slid her fingers into Cole's soft curls and rode his talented tongue.

Her abdominal muscles tensed, and her entire body stiffened as she cried out his name, over and over, until her throat felt raw and she shattered into tiny, glittering pieces. Renee's chest heaved as Cole finally lifted his head, his lips and chin shiny with the evidence of her pleasure.

He pressed kisses to her inner thigh, then to her belly. And before she could catch her breath, Cole slid inside her. The sound of his skin slapping against hers and his low, determined grunts filled the space around them.

Ren gazed up at the gorgeous man hovering over her. He was focused. Beads of sweat formed on his forehead. His quiet moans of pleasure grew more intense, as did her soft murmurs. Cole rolled his hips, seemingly determined to make her feel him from every single angle. She'd hardly had a chance to come down from the intense high of the orgasm he'd given her. Yet he was taking her there again.

When Cole's gaze met hers, there was something in his eyes. Something he wanted to say but wouldn't allow himself to. He threaded his fingers through hers, lifting their joined hands above her head. His kiss was deep and passionate. His mouth was salty with the taste of her.

The friction of his pelvis moving against hers intensified the ecstasy building low in her belly.

An overwhelming sensation began building deep in her core, radiated up her spine and catapulted her into bliss, his name on her lips. She held onto him, as if he'd float away if she didn't anchor his solid body to hers.

Suddenly, Cole's muscles tensed and his back stiffened as he reached his own pinnacle. He whispered her name in a breathy moan again and again.

Cole kissed her, then collapsed onto the bed beside her. He gathered her to his heaving chest, folding one arm behind his head as he stared up at the ceiling.

There was an awkwardness they hadn't experienced before. Now things were weird between them because she'd broken the rules they'd established.

Ren traced the fine hair that trailed down his belly with light fingertips and frowned, her face buried in his chest. "What I said earlier… I shouldn't have said that. It's not what we agreed to."

"Don't apologize for asking for what you want, sweetheart." Cole lifted her chin, so their eyes met. "And don't think I don't have feelings for you, Ren. I do. I just… I'm not…"

"I know." She pressed her cheek to his chest again. "It was such a beautiful, emotional ceremony. I just got caught up in the moment. Please, let's not talk about it anymore."

Ren squeezed her eyes shut, hoping Cole wouldn't notice her silent tears.

Cole wrapped his arms around Ren and dropped a soft kiss on top of her head before lying back against the pillow. He stared at the ceiling again, his pulse racing as Ren's words replayed in his head.

Make love to me, Cole. Like I'm yours. Like this thing we have is real.

Cole rubbed a hand up and down the soft, dewy skin on her arm. His heart ached as he recalled Ren's pained smile. Her lips had said it was no big deal but the disappointment in her eyes nearly broke him.

He never wanted to hurt Ren. But she obviously wanted more from this relationship.

There was no denying that he'd gotten caught up in his feelings for Ren and Mercer. But a serious, long-term relationship wasn't what they'd agreed to. It wasn't what he'd been looking for. Because he enjoyed the freedom of being the eternal bachelor.

Or maybe you're just scared.

Cole tried to shake off the thought, but he could feel wetness on his skin.

Ren *was* crying silent tears, which meant she didn't want him to know.

Cole wanted to give her anything she desired to make those tears stop. But he cared too much for Ren to mislead her.

Yes, he had feelings for her. And yes, he believed he could be happy with Ren. Yet, there was some part of him that was terrified of the prospect and worried that he wasn't good enough for Ren and Mercer. Because they deserved the world.

"I adore you, Ren. You know that, right?" Cole kissed her forehead.

"Yes." Ren nodded, her cheek slipping against the wetness on his chest. She swiped her eyes and cleared her throat. "I feel the same."

Cole sighed, then rubbed her arm. "I'd better take care of this."

He went to the bathroom, but when he returned, Ren was gone. As were her clothes that had been piled on the chair.

"Ren?" He walked through the door to her hotel room.

"I'm here." Ren emerged from her bathroom dressed in a pair of leggings, a racing top and sneakers. She ran her fingers through her hair. Reminding him of how he'd sifted her strands through his fingers as she lay in his arms the night before.

"You're leaving?"

"I'm too amped to go to sleep. I'm going to run on the treadmill in the gym."

"We should talk, Ren," he said. "I'll go with you."

"Thank you, but I think I need a little time alone. Besides, I think maybe I'm becoming a little too reliant on you, you know?"

Cole frowned, his chest tightening. "I like doing things for you and Mercer."

"I know." She gave him a soft smile. "It's one of the many things I love about you. But right now, I just need a little space."

"If that's what you want." He pulled her into a hug. "But I'm here whenever you need me."

Ren pulled out of his embrace. "Don't wait up for me. I'm not sure how long I'll be, and I'll probably just crash in my bed tonight."

"Ren." Cole caught her hand and she turned to face him. "We're good, right?"

"Of course." She smiled, but there was pain in her eyes. She lifted onto her toes and gave him a quick kiss. "See you in the morning." She gave him a little wave, then left.

Cole returned to his room and shut the connecting door. Maybe he'd fucked up by agreeing to this experiment with Renee. Maybe it would've been better for all of them if he'd said no and meant it. But having Ren and Mercer in his life had brought him a happiness he hadn't realized he'd been missing.

So he couldn't regret the past few months they'd spent together. And he'd do whatever it took to salvage their relationship. Because going back to life without Ren and Mercer just wasn't an option.

Twenty-Two

Breakfast the next morning was quiet and uneventful. Ren and Cole shared warm, cordial conversation about the wedding, the hotel and about a sensory toy she wanted to get for Mercer. They talked about anything but what had happened last night.

It was a mistake. And it wasn't fair to Cole. She realized that, but she couldn't help the way she felt about him, either. She didn't just love Cole as a friend; she was in love with him. If she was being really honest with herself, she'd fallen in love with Cole long before she'd asked him to agree to their experiment.

When she returned home, Mercer was down for a nap. Her mom took one look at her and knew something was wrong. She had one question: had Cole done anything to hurt her? When Renee said no, her mother opened her arms and she fell into them, crying like a baby. Her mother was kind enough not to press her for details. She appreciated that.

The next day, her mom hung around to keep an eye on Mercer while Ren went out into the field with a master gardener she'd hired as a consultant. They were making the rounds and checking on all the crops: blueberries and strawberries; shallots, tomatoes, cucumbers, beans and carrots; Swiss chard, several varieties of lettuce and kale.

Everything looked lovely, and the beans, lettuce and a few other plants were already starting to produce. Next, she would be meeting with Jeb and Leonard Dawson about building a chicken pen and roost.

But first, she needed to make lunch for her picky little eater. Today she was making one of his favorite meals: homemade chicken and dumplings. The house smelled heavenly.

"Merce?" Ren stayed calm as she looked all over for Mercer, despite the slight panic building in her chest. She tried her best to watch him like a hawk but it only took a moment for her curious little boy to get into something.

She found him lying underneath her desk. He sucked his thumb as he stared up.

"There you are." Ren got on her knees and tickled Mercer's belly, making him laugh. "What is it that you find so fascinating underneath my desk?"

Mercer pointed up, so Ren lay on her back underneath the desk beside him. He was pointing at an engraved silver plate Ren hadn't even known was there.

"That's why Aunt Willie always dusted underneath the desk, too," Ren muttered quietly to herself. She lifted onto her elbows so she could read the words engraved on the plate.

To my lovely Wilhelmina. A gift for our wedding day.

A date was inscribed beneath the words: September 16, 1972.

Wedding date?

Her Aunt Wilhelmina had never married. Had she planned to wed Eduardo, the man she'd had her bad boy experiment with? If so, what had gone wrong?

"C'mon, Bug." Ren scooted from beneath the desk and climbed to her feet. "I made your favorite—chicken and dumplings." A wide smile spread on the little boy's face, as he grabbed her hand.

They washed their hands, then Mercer climbed into his booster seat. His bowl was filled with the tender, juicy strips of chicken and the cooled dumplings, which he could eat with his favorite fork. He didn't care for the broth.

Ren sat beside him with her bowl, but she wasn't hungry. She couldn't help wondering what had happened between Aunt Wilhelmina and Eduardo. Had he changed his mind? Had she? Or had they come to realize their relationship was better off as it was?

She couldn't help thinking of Cole. Ren hadn't seen him since they'd returned from Max and Quinn's wedding. He'd sent her sweet little text messages to check on her and Mercer and see if they needed anything. Her reply was always gracious and warm. And she ended by typing: Talk soon. Because eventually they would. She just wasn't ready to talk now.

Cole hadn't done anything wrong. He'd simply kept to their agreement. She was the one who'd broken the rules by falling in love with him. Ren wanted Cole in her life, even if all he was offering was friendship. But she'd been devastated by the realization that she loved him as more than a friend, but he didn't love her back. It would take some time to come to terms with that.

Mercer reached out and touched her face. It was only then she realized tears were sliding down her cheeks.

"It's okay, sweetie." Ren wiped the tears away and forced a big smile. She kissed the little boy's forehead. "Mommy's fine. I promise."

But they both knew the truth. Mommy wasn't fine.

That night, after her mother had left for Knoxville, Ren put Mercer to bed, beneath the little tent Cole had created for him. He was clutching the sensory teddy bear Cole had bought him a few weeks ago.

Ren returned to her bedroom after her shower. She glanced at the spot on the floor where she was sitting when she'd first kissed Cole a few months ago and sighed. It felt like there wasn't a single place in this house that didn't remind her of Cole. As she put on her pajamas and prepared to get into bed, she noticed the box beneath her bed sticking out.

Mercer had evidently been under her bed again.

Ren reached for the box, to shove it back beneath the bed, but she couldn't help noticing the book safe. Over the past few months, she'd tried street addresses, family members' birthdates and every important date she could think of as the combination. Nothing had worked.

But now she had a new date to try. The date Aunt Wilhelmina had planned to get married.

Ren sat on the floor with her legs folded and tried to remember the date inscribed beneath the desk. September 16, 1972. She pulled out the little safe and carefully dialed each number: nine, one, six. When she lifted the lid, the book safe creaked open.

Ren set it on the floor and scanned the contents. It contained two stacks of letters tied with ribbon, addressed to Aunt Wilhelmina from Eduardo Cordeiro. The box also contained two more journals. The first picked up from where the last journal she'd read had left off. Ren opened the leatherbound book and started to read.

She read late into the night until she'd finished the first journal, in which she discovered that, like her, her great-aunt had fallen in love with the subject of her experiment. But Eduardo had fallen in love with Wilhelmina, too. They'd planned to secretly get married and tell their families—whom they feared wouldn't have approved—later.

In the second journal, she discovered that Eduardo had wanted to save a little nest egg before they married. He didn't want Aunt Willie's family, which owned lots of land and was doing well financially at the time, to think he was marrying Wilhelmina for her money. He took a job as the captain of a tuna fishing boat. It was dangerous work, but he was well paid. But two weeks before they were to be married, Eduardo's boat sank in a huge storm off the New England coast, killing him and everyone on board.

Her great-aunt had been devastated. Not only because of losing the man she loved, but because she was pregnant with their child. She'd wanted to raise the child on her own, but when she'd finally confessed everything to Aunt Bea, her sister had convinced her it would be best if she gave the child up. Her great-aunt's journal entries ended soon after she'd left for California, where she would have her child and give it up for adoption. Ren shut the journal, devastated by Aunt Wilhelmina's tragic love story. Eduardo had reciprocated her aunt's feelings, and still their story hadn't had a happy ending.

Ren carefully replaced the items in the book safe. Then she set it on top of her dresser. A daily, visible reminder that, with the exception of her grandparents, the Lockwood family history was filled with failed relationships and tragic love stories.

She cared deeply for Cole. But he'd been right about not risking their friendship for a fling. She needed to cut her romantic ties to Cole and salvage their friendship.

Because bad boy experiments never ended well.

Twenty-Three

Cole pulled the Ram TRX into the driveway of his grandfather's cabin just outside of town. It was the place Grandpa Joe had planned to live out the rest of his life with their grandmother—the love of his life. But fate had been cruel, and not long after he'd officially turned the reins of King's Finest over to Cole's dad, their grandmother had been diagnosed with terminal cancer. She'd only gotten to spend a few months truly enjoying the old place.

Once, Cole had asked his grandfather why he hadn't sold the cabin with all the bad memories of his grandmother being sick. He'd simply smiled and said, "Your grandmother likes it here, so this is where we'll stay." He'd never asked about it again. But he had to admit that whenever he visited, it reminded him of his sweet grandmother, too. How she'd loved nature and animals. And how much she loved going out on the lake.

Before Cole reached the front door, Grandpa Joe opened it.

"How'd you know I was here?" Cole asked.

"I can still hear pretty good." The old man chuckled. "You can hear that thing coming down the road from a mile away with that souped-up engine of yours."

Fair point.

"You wanted to see me, Gramps. Thinking of renovating the old place?" Cole glanced around the cabin. The kitchen was a little dated, but everything was still in good shape. It was nothing that would bother his grandfather. Unless… "You're not selling the cabin, are you?"

"They'll be carrying me out of here feet first." His grandfather eyed him.

"Okay, Pops. Forget I mentioned it." Cole chuckled. "What can I do for you, sir?"

"Actually, this is about what I can do for you." His grandfather rubbed his chin, his expression suddenly serious. "Can I get you a drink?"

"Got a beer?"

"Sure 'nuff." His grandfather grabbed two beers from the small fridge behind the bar, then joined Cole on the sofa. They opened their beers and sipped them in silence. Finally, his grandfather spoke, a pained look in his eyes. "I owe you an apology, son."

"For what?" Cole turned toward his grandfather.

Grandpa Joe sighed heavily. "When you decided you didn't want to go to college, I thought you were just being lazy. I didn't understand the struggles you were having with school. I should've been more supportive. But at the time, I thought you just needed a little tough love. That's why I gave you the ultimatum that if you didn't go to college, you couldn't work in the company. I thought it'd push you to go to school like your brothers. To tap into all of the potential I've always known was there."

"We don't need to talk about this again, Gramps." Cole frowned, taking another sip of his beer.

"Yes, we do." The old man emphasized each word, his voice shaky. "Because the ultimatum was my idea, and I was wrong. And when Milo Lockwood took you under his wing and you were helping him build his business, I was hot under the collar. It felt like a rejection of our family and everything we've built with King's Finest."

"It wasn't. I just knew college wasn't right for me then. Being forced out of the company made me grow up and figure things out. Like what it was I was good at and enjoyed doing. When Milo gave me a shot as his apprentice… I found my place in the world. It wasn't about you at all, Gramps."

"Guess that's part of the problem." His grandfather pushed his smudged glasses up the bridge of his nose. "You made your decision without regard for the family or the company I'd been working to build since I was sixteen years old. At the time, I thought that was damn selfish of you."

"You aren't alone in that," Cole said, thinking of his brother Max.

"Maybe. But I was wrong to begrudge your decision to go out on your own and do what makes you happy, son. You've done far better for yourself than any of us could've imagined. And I can't tell you how incredibly proud of you I am for that, son." Grandpa Joe patted Cole's knee, his voice filled with love and pride.

"Thanks, Gramps. That means a lot."

"I'll let you in on a little secret." His grandfather set down his beer and turned to Cole more fully. "The reason I took you walking away from the company so hard is because from the time you were just a wee thing… you were the one who most reminded me of me." He chuckled. "You looked just like me. You had my confidence and swagger. My smart-ass mouth." They both laughed. "I'd envisioned you leading the company into the future long after I'm gone."

"But I'm the fourth in line," Cole said.

"Don't matter." His grandfather chuckled. "You're the visionary of the family. You've got drive and ingenuity. You're a natural-born leader and one hell of a businessman. Look at what you've done with your own company. Was I wrong?"

"Guess not." Cole drained the last of his beer. "But Blake's doing a hell of a job. He'll make a great CEO when the time comes."

"He is, and he will indeed," Grandpa Joe agreed. "I'm mighty proud of him and of *all* of you, son," Grandpa Joe reiterated.

"Thanks, Gramps." Cole bumped a gentle shoulder against his grandfather's.

"I just wish your grandmother had lived to see how

everything turned out." The old man heaved a sigh as he ran a hand over his smooth head. "Dixon Bazemore and I were talking about that at the wedding. It was a beautiful, heartfelt ceremony. A happy day for both of our families. But it hurt like hell that our girls didn't live to see the day our two grandchildren would stand up there at that altar and get married."

"I've been thinking a lot about Gram, too. I wish she could've been there."

"Dixon gave Quinn two of his wife's most treasured jewelry pieces. Her engagement ring, which became part of Quinn's engagement ring. And the diamond necklace Dixon gave his wife for their fiftieth anniversary. Quinn wore it during the ceremony. It was a great way to make his late wife part of his granddaughter's wedding day." Gramps sighed. "I wish I'd had the foresight to do something like that for your brothers' and sister's weddings. I didn't, but I won't make the same mistake with you." He waggled a finger.

"Hate to disappoint you, Pops, but there isn't a wedding in my future."

It was the kind of statement Cole usually made smugly. But saying it now made his chest feel hollow. Like there was a hole where his heart should be.

"Isn't there?" His grandfather furrowed his wiry brows. "'Cause you've sure seemed sweet on Milo's granddaughter these past few months."

Cole frowned, his throat suddenly dry.

"Ren is great. Smart, beautiful, sweet, hardworking, determined...she can be stubborn as hell." He laughed bitterly, then sighed. "But she and her son…they deserve someone…I don't know…*better* than me, I guess."

"And what *exactly* would make someone better for her, Cole?"

"Renee is a brilliant scientist with double PhDs. She's made important discoveries that are having a real impact in the world, and I'm…"

"A brilliant businessman who has forged his own path. You're building an empire, Cole. Creating your very own legacy. Impacting this town and this state in real, measurable ways. More importantly, you care deeply for Renee and her child. I see it in your eyes whenever you're with them." His grandfather smiled. "Reminds me of the way my eyes lit up whenever I was around your grandmother. The question is, what are you going to do about it?"

"I've been on my own so long, Gramps. What if I'm not capable of changing?"

"Has Renee asked you to change?"

"No, of course not."

"Then why do you think she expects you to?" His grandfather folded his arms.

"I'm not a traditional kind of guy."

"That dog won't hunt," his grandfather said. "Renee was married to a 'traditional kind of guy.' Didn't work out too well. Maybe what she needs is someone unconventional. Whatever you think your faults are, Cole, you're a good man, son. You've been there for Renee, helping her through this every step of the way. Even though you want that land for yourself." Gramps squeezed his arm. "Not many men—not even good ones—would do that. It's obvious you love the girl."

"I do." Cole didn't hesitate. For the past few days he'd been pondering the depth of his feelings for her. Just as before, his relationship with Renee had touched him in a way no one else ever had. "I love Ren and Mercer. I'd do anything for them. That's why I want what's best for them. Even if that isn't me."

"Seems to me, you make them just as happy as they make you. And I'd venture that there ain't a man out there who'll care for them, protect them and love them the way you do. They're pretty damn lucky to have you in their lives."

Cole's grandfather's words hit him. Made him think of all the times he'd shared with Renee and Mercer. And of all the things he'd done to ensure they were safe and happy. He thought of all the emotions that had been building in his chest these past months. And how miserable he'd been without them these past few days.

Commitment had always seemed scary. Because what if he screwed up? What if he chose the wrong person? He loved his family, and they'd resolved their differences. But their failure to understand him and to accept him for who he was earlier in his life…it had scarred him. Made him feel as if he was the only person he could rely on. The only person he could trust.

But as he sat there now, all he could think of was how devastated he would be if Ren and Mercer walked out of his life. That loss was a much scarier prospect than any of his concerns about entering a long-term commitment.

"Thanks, Gramps." Cole hugged his grandfather, then stood quickly. "I need to talk to Renee."

She'd been avoiding him since they'd come back from Max and Quinn's wedding, when he'd blown it by not telling her how he really felt. He hadn't wanted to push. But now he really needed to speak with her. To be honest about his feelings.

"That a boy. But there's one more thing…the reason I invited you here." His grandfather chuckled, slowly rising to his feet, too. "Can't give you the business, but I can give you something else." He reached behind the bar and produced a small box.

"What's this?" Cole slid open the old matchbox and studied its contents. "Gramps, is this…? I can't—"

"Yes, you can." Grandpa Joe patted his shoulder. "Hope it brings you as much luck as it brought us."

Cole bearhugged his grandfather. "Thanks, Gramps."

"All right, all right. Don't you have somewhere you need to be right now?"

"Yes, sir." Cole shoved the box Grandpa Joe had given him into his pocket, then clapped a hand on the old man's shoulder. "I do."

He had to see Ren. But there were two stops he needed to make first.

Twenty-Four

Renee sat at her desk sorting through the invoices to be paid. For now, there were plenty of expenses and zero income. But she'd done her research and was prepared to absorb the costs. She'd banked enough to keep the farm going for at least a year without tapping into her savings.

Still, her plan was coming along nicely. The plants were healthy and strong, and several of the small crops had begun to bear fruit. The chicken enclosure and roost had been built, and she was now the proud mama of a small flock of baby chicks. She smiled, thinking of how sweet and gentle Mercer had been with the tiny little bundles of yellow fuzz. It would be about six months before they'd be ready to begin laying eggs. In the meantime, he'd get to bond with them.

Ren glanced up at the sound of Cole's Ram TRX pulling into his driveway. Mercer was asleep, or else he'd have his little face pressed to the office window saying *Vroom*.

Every evening when she heard Cole come home, she practically held her breath.

Part of her hoped Cole wouldn't knock on her door. Part of her hoped he would.

Ren sat frozen after the slam of the truck door, her heart beating a bit faster as she strained to hear the crunch of gravel beneath his feet as he took the path between their houses. But after a few minutes, there was only silence.

Renee nibbled on her lower lip and heaved a sigh. When her cell phone started playing "(Sittin' On) the Dock of the Bay" by Otis Redding, it startled her. A photo of her grandfather with his wide grin filled the screen, accompanying his favorite song. She checked her watch. It was after eight in the evening. Her grandfather had usually settled in to watch his favorite TV shows for the night. He and her grandmother rarely called at this hour.

"Hey, Grandad. Everything okay?"

"It is, sweetheart. For you, especially." He chuckled.

"I don't understand."

"Cole pulled his bid for the property, so if you still want the farm, it's yours. Congratulations."

"I don't understand," Ren repeated. "When did this happen?"

"He left here about an hour ago."

Ren sat frozen, barely able to believe what her grandfather was saying.

Why would Cole withdraw his bid after investing months of work into this deal?

"Thought you'd be happy to hear the news," her grandfather said, his voice tinged with concern. "This is still what you want, isn't it?"

"Yes, of course. I'm thrilled by the news, Grandad. Really. I'm just…surprised, that's all." Ren got up from the desk. She rubbed the back of her neck as she paced the floor, glancing out the window toward Cole's house. "Did Cole say *why* he withdrew his offer?"

There was a pause more pregnant than Zora.

"You won, sweetheart," her grandfather said finally. "So why does it matter why?"

"I don't know, Gramps." Ren's voice broke and her vision clouded. She sucked in a deep breath, then sighed. "It just does."

"Cole said he had a change of heart. That he agreed with you about the farm being part of our family's legacy. He said that after watching you work so passionately to revive the farm, he realized it was in good hands. He doesn't want to interfere with that. In fact, once he completes the renovations on Bea's house, he'll sell the place to you at a fair price, if that's what you want."

Cole was going to sell her the place?

In the beginning, that was exactly what she'd hoped for. But now, she couldn't imagine not looking out her window and knowing he was there.

"What about his plans to build his luxury community?"

"Says he'll build a scaled-down version on the plot of land that was his second option. And he's going to push the county to hurry those plans to replace that bridge into town, since it'll impact his new development. So it's a win for everyone."

"And exactly what you've been hoping for." Renee laughed softly. "You always were a sly old devil when it came to getting Cole to do the right thing. I see it's still working."

"What makes you think he changed his mind because of me?" her grandfather asked. "And what makes you think Cole is the only one I use those tricks on?" Her grandfather chuckled again. "Now, I have to go. Your grandmother paused our favorite show so I could make this call, and now she's giving me that evil eye of hers."

"I am not! We love you, sweetheart!" her grandmother shouted in the background. "Congratulations!"

"Thanks, Gran!" Ren bade them good-night and ended the call.

She sat back against her chair, one hand over her mouth. Her heart thudded in her chest. She'd done it. The rest was just a formality. Ren would soon be the owner of the land that had been in her family for three generations. And she planned to restore it and make it even better. Something that would last another three generations. A legacy for her son and any other children she might have.

Not that there were any prospects of that.

Ren walked over to the window facing Cole's house. It was about half an hour before sunset and the sky was beautiful, streaked with pinks and oranges, the silhouette of the Smoky Mountains in the distance. This felt right. Being here in Magnolia Lake on her family's land…this was *exactly* where she and Mercer belonged.

So why did she feel heartbroken?

You know exactly why.

Ren toyed with the locket on her neck. It was the only jewelry from her ex-husband she still wore, because it held the most adorable photo of Mercer as a baby.

She couldn't stop thinking of what Cole had done. The sacrifice he'd made.

"You really miss him, don't you, honey?" Her mother's soft voice came from behind her.

Ren nodded, looking out of the window longingly.

Evelyn stood beside her and slipped an arm around her waist, their heads together. "Mercer does, too. He comes to this window all the time and says, *Vroom*!"

Fat tears fell on Ren's cheeks. She swiped at them angrily. "This is all my fault. I shouldn't have pushed him into this experiment. Then we'd still be friends, and everyone would be happy."

"You were never happy just being Cole's friend, honey." Her mom wiped her tears. "You were just willing to accept his friendship."

Ren pressed a hand to her mouth, the tears falling harder. Her mother was right. She'd been lying to herself and to Cole from the very start when she'd declared she'd only wanted a physical relationship.

"Cole didn't walk away from you, honey. You're the one who asked for space. So go talk to him. This time, be honest about how you feel. At least he'll know the truth and you two can decide where to go from there."

Her mother hugged her and patted her back. "I'm going to bed. But I'm here, and I've got Mercer. So if I don't see you later tonight… I'll see you in the morning." Her mother smiled, then walked toward the stairs.

Ren stood there, unsure of what she should do. Her heart ached at the thought of another rejection from Cole. But what was the point of an experiment, except to keep trying different approaches until you found the one that worked?

She hurried up the stairs and prepared to do just that.

Cole stood back and admired the paint job in his new master bedroom suite. His crew had done the work of remodeling the bedroom and adding an en suite bathroom. They'd done meticulous tilework in the bathroom and refinished the plaster in the old house. But he'd wanted to paint this room himself.

Milo had started him off as a painter when he was just a kid. Every now and again, he liked to do a paint job in one of the long-term flips he lived in, to remember how he'd started.

Cole cleaned the rollers in the sink. Then he stripped off his grimy clothing and took a long, hot shower. He lathered his body and washed the grit from his hair.

Cole turned off the water and heard a faint knocking sound. He stood still and listened but didn't hear it again. God, he hoped it wasn't the plumbing in this old house. He hadn't budgeted for that in the renovation plan. Cole toweled himself off, then walked into the bedroom. He couldn't help glancing over at Ren's house. Her bedroom light wasn't on.

Then he noticed movement below. It was Ren. She had her phone to her ear as she took the path from his place back to hers. He knocked on the window, but she didn't hear him. Cole huffed.

Maybe Ren had just come to say thank you because he'd retracted his bid on the property. Or maybe she'd come to say she was prepared to resume their friendship but wanted nothing more. He hoped like hell it was Option #3.

There was only one way to find out.

Cole glanced around his bedroom, which was a mess after the painting and remodeling. Then he gazed over at the balcony off Ren's bedroom. His mouth curved in a smile.

It was probably a terrible idea. But Ren was an amazing woman and his best friend. He loved her and Mercer, and he'd screwed up by not telling Ren that when he'd had the chance. So he was prepared to go big, because Ren deserved one more grand gesture.

Ren poured herself a little of the King's Finest peach brandy that she kept stocked for her mother. She'd gone over to Cole's house, knowing he was there. She'd knocked three times, and had even tried calling him, but he hadn't answered.

Was Cole upset about giving up the land deal?

Her phone rang, and a photo she'd taken of Cole and Mercer filled her screen, both of their faces stretched wide with happy grins that made her smile every time she saw it.

Ren answered the phone as quickly as she could. “Cole, hi.”

“Hello, sweetheart.” She could hear the smile in his voice. “It’s so good to hear your voice again.”

“Yours, too.” Ren nodded, her eyes pricking with tears. “Cole, I’m so sorry. I—”

“Why don’t you come to your balcony door and tell me all about it.”

“You climbed the trellis?” she asked, but he’d already ended the call. “Hello?”

Ren hurried up to her room and opened the balcony door. Cole was standing there with a wide grin.

“What were you thinking?” Ren slapped his arm. “You could’ve fallen and hurt yourself.”

“That should tell you how badly I needed to see you, beautiful.” Cole stroked her cheek, his eyes filled with a warmth that seeped into her skin.

She’d missed this man. Missed her lover and her friend. The days they’d been apart felt like an eternity.

Ren held a finger up to her lips and tugged Cole inside her room. She closed the balcony door. “Why did you need to see me?”

“I was in the shower when you came over to my place. I knocked on the window as you were leaving, but you didn’t hear me.” He squeezed her hand. “Why’d you come to see me?”

“To thank you for what you did by walking away from the deal. And for what you told my grandfather about the farm being in good hands with me. I don’t know what prompted you to walk away but—”

"Yes, you do." Cole's mouth quirked in a half smile as he cupped her cheek. His dark eyes locked with hers.

"So you really did walk away from the deal for me." Ren studied Cole's face. "I can't thank you enough. This means everything to me."

"And you, Ren, mean everything to me."

Ren's heart squeezed in her chest, and her eyes stung with tears for the second time tonight.

"I have a confession to make." Ren wrapped her arms around herself. "When I said I would be satisfied with a no-strings, casual relationship, I was lying to you and to myself." She sighed. "Because it isn't true. I am very much in love with you, Cole. I think I always have been."

He pulled her closer, a soft smile curving his sensuous lips. "Do you know why I agreed to this experiment of yours?"

"Because you were afraid I'd start seeing Leonard Dawson?" She grinned. "Spoiler alert—I wouldn't have."

"Okay, that was part of it," he admitted with a chuckle, then sighed. "Imagining you with someone else… Honestly, Ren, it was pure torture. And since you came back, I haven't wanted to be with anyone but you. It was kind of a new concept for me. So I needed to understand why."

"Did you find your answer?" Ren looped her arms around Cole's neck as she gazed up at him.

"I did." Cole cradled her face. "Because I'm in love with you, too. And for me, no other woman in the world compares to you, Ren. These past few months, we've built a genuine friendship and become an important part of each other's lives. The highlight of my week is the time I get to spend with you and Mercer. Because I'm happier with both of you in my life. I don't ever want to go back to a life that doesn't include you. Because the two of you..." His voice was shaky and his eyes filled with emotion. "You *and* Mercer mean everything to me now. And I don't *ever* want that to change."

"Really?" Ren's glasses were foggy, and tears of joy rolled down her cheeks.

"Really." Cole lifted her chin. "I love you and Mercer, Ren. And I want us to be a family...officially." He clutched her hand as he met her gaze. "Marry me."

"What?" She stared at him, wide-eyed. Her heart felt as if it was beating out of her chest. "You're not serious...are you?"

Cole reached into the back pocket of his jeans and pulled out a ring box. He opened it, revealing a gorgeous vintage sapphire-and-diamond art deco–style engagement ring.

Ren gasped and pressed her fingertips to her mouth. "Cole. It's beautiful."

"This ring belonged to my grandmother, Ren. My grandfather gave it to me because, like my mother and sister, he realized how very much I am in love with you. That being with you makes me happier than I have ever been. It just took me a minute to work through my issues and to realize how much I want a life with you."

Cole removed the ring from the box and turned it so she could read the inscription inside.

To my darling, Ren. I love you forever and always.

"It's perfect." Warm tears streamed down her face.

Cole pressed a soft, lingering kiss to her mouth.

"Marry me, Ren. Please. Because you mean the world to me. And I don't ever want to be without you again."

"Yes, I'll marry you, Cole." Ren nodded, tears flowing down her face. "Because I don't ever want to be without you again, either."

Cole captured her mouth in a kiss.

Tears ran down her face, and her heart felt full, even as a zing of electricity shot down her spine, setting every nerve ending in her body on fire.

The kiss was filled with love: passionate, yet tender. It was everything she wanted. Because *Cole* was everything she wanted.

Epilogue

Three and a half months later

Cole stepped out of his Jaguar F-Type and handed the valet the keys. King's Finest Family Restaurant was a family-style restaurant, so valets wouldn't be the norm. But Savannah, Quinn and Iris had thought it would be fun to do a formal grand opening, complete with a red carpet and Tennessee celebrities like Dade Willis, whose latest song was blazing up the country charts.

A line had already begun to form on the sidewalk outside the restaurant—a full hour before the doors opened to the public. Both locals and out-of-towners were eager to be part of King's Finest Family Restaurant.

Cole handed the valet his keys, then offered his fiancée his hand, helping her out of the car. Ren looked gorgeous in a sleeveless black jumpsuit with a flouncy ruffle down one side and black ballet flats. They stopped, smiling for the photographers, before continuing inside.

"Have I told you that the second you put that thing on, I haven't been able to think of anything but how quickly I'll be able to get you out of it?"

"Cole Abbott." Ren elbowed him, laughing. "This is a *family* restaurant."

"Okay, all right," he grumbled. "But we're staying two hours tops. Then you, me and that sexy-ass black jumpsuit have a date back at my place."

"You're on." She squeezed his hand.

Cole dropped a kiss on Ren's lips, and she smiled.

"You two again with the PDA?" Parker clutched Kayleigh's hand. His brother wore a black suit and tie. He pushed his black eyeglasses up the bridge of his nose.

"Pay no mind to the PDA police here. You two are adorable." Kayleigh shook her head. Her red curls, pulled into a high ponytail, waved behind her.

She wore a pretty black dress with an unusual design. "My husband's bark is worse than his bite." Kayleigh tapped Parker's chest with her crystal-studded black leather Alexander McQueen bag.

"This place looks incredible, Cole." Parker glanced around at the interior of the restaurant.

"I can hardly believe this was once my run-down old jewelry-and-consignment shop." Kayleigh took in the wall of floor-to-ceiling windows that spanned the front of the restaurant, bathing the space with natural light.

Cole's construction team had done a hell of a job on the restoration of the building. The exposed brick paid homage to the original restaurant owned by his maternal grandpa Gus. The seating was a mix of high-top tables, traditional tables and bench seating—all designed by his brother-in-law and built locally by Dallas's company, Hamilton Haus.

Quinn had worked feverishly with local tradesmen, retailers and farmers to source the lighting and other design materials as well as all of the food they served. Ren's farm would be the source for many of the restaurant's organic fruits and vegetables starting the following year.

The shelves were stocked with spirits from King's Finest and other local distilleries. The wines were supplied by a variety of local vineyards.

"I'm proud of the way it all turned out." Cole led his siblings through the space, giving them a mini-tour of the restaurant. "Most importantly, I'm glad that Mom is pleased with it. This is her baby."

"Look at her. She's beaming," Kayleigh said. "I can't wait to see the plans for my inn."

"It'll be amazing, of course." Cole grinned.

The inn was slated to be built for Kayleigh the following year. It would be situated on a plot of land once owned by her family and recently gifted back to her by his father, Duke.

After the tour, they gathered at the back of the restaurant where Iris was putting some final touches on the stage decorations.

Zora was videoconferencing Dallas's mother, Tish, who was watching their infant daughter, Ella.

"Ella is so adorable." Ren pressed a hand to her chest. "She looks just like you, Zora. Yet, she has many of her dad's features."

"She's the perfect combination." Zora smiled at Dallas lovingly.

"Just like us, babe." Dallas kissed his wife.

"More of the PDA?" Parker complained.

Zora elbowed her brother in the ribs, and he laughed.

"Thank you all for coming a little earlier," Duke said, his arm around his wife's waist. "I thought it would be nice if we had a private family toast before the restaurant opens."

Their mother looked gorgeous in a sparkly, floor-length dress in a deep burgundy. And she was beaming with pride.

"You all know how much this venture means to me. I just wanted to thank you all for your support and your contributions in making this happen," Iris said. "But nothing makes me happier than seeing each of you having found your soulmates and starting families of your own. And I honestly couldn't have picked more perfect matches for each of you, if I'd tried. And believe me, I tried."

They all laughed as one of the servers brought them all glasses of champagne.

"Duke and I are truly blessed to have all of you in our lives," Iris continued, her eyes welling with tears.

"Thank you so much, Iris." Savannah hugged her and everyone else chimed in their thanks, too.

"I was an only child and so was Duke," Grandpa Joe said. "We wanted more kids but couldn't have them. So I would never have imagined that I'd one day be surrounded by family like this." His grandfather got choked up and placed a hand over his heart. "I love each and every one of you, more than words can say."

"So before your mother and grandfather start with the waterworks again..." his father teased, handing Iris a drink. "I'd like to propose a toast."

He raised his glass, and everyone else did, too.

"To your mother—the most incredible woman I've ever known. Thank you for your love, patience and wisdom. And for supporting me and King's Finest all these years. It is our honor to now support you as you pursue your dreams." Duke turned toward the rest of them. "And to this group of amazing, accomplished people who I am so proud to know and even prouder to call family. Whether our bond is by blood or marriage, we are truly grateful to have you in our lives."

His father's voice broke with emotion, and everyone teased him. He laughed, wiping the corners of his eyes. "Thank you for being part of our world. I can't wait to see all that you have yet to accomplish. To family."

"To family." They echoed, holding their glasses up and clinking them together.

"Now, I want you all to see the menu." Iris nodded to one of the servers who unveiled the large menu board on the wall.

They'd known she'd planned to incorporate their family's recipes and share them with the world. But they hadn't known that their names would be incorporated into each of the signature dishes they'd either contributed or inspired—including Ren's Chicken and Dumplings, Cole's Slaw Burger, Quinn's Peach Cobbler, Parker's Old Fashioned and Zora's One-Two Punch.

It was a surprise to all of them and a testament to their mother's love for her family.

"That was incredibly sweet of your mom." Ren dabbed beneath her eyes, trying her best not to ruin her makeup. "I can't believe she included me. Our wedding isn't until next summer."

"You and Mercer are already family, babe." Cole kissed the hand that bore his grandmother's engagement ring.

An older man approached him. "Excuse me, are you Cole Abbott?"

Cole didn't know the man, but something about him seemed familiar. "Yes, sir. But the restaurant still isn't open to the public for another…twenty minutes."

"I know," the man said. "But I was hoping the two of us could talk."

"Can I help you with something?" Cole asked.

"Actually, I was hoping we could help each other."

Cole raised a brow and exchanged a look with Ren. He assessed the man. "I'm sorry, but now isn't the best time to talk business. This is a special night for our family. Especially for my mother." He pulled a card from his wallet and handed it to the man. "Why don't you call my office next week?"

The man studied the card for a moment and then smiled, as if he knew something Cole didn't. It made him uneasy. He slipped his hand into Ren's, threading their fingers.

"Actually, that's why I came here tonight. I thought it would be the best time to introduce myself to the entire family." The man's light brown skin crinkled around his eyes.

Cole couldn't shake the feeling he'd seen him somewhere before. "And why is that, Mr....?"

"Valentine." A deep, almost mischievous smile curved one side of the man's mouth. "*Abbott* Valentine of Valentine Vineyards."

"Ahh." Cole nodded knowingly. "If this is about supplying the restaurant… I'm pretty sure my mother and sister-in-law have already lined up all of their vendors for now."

"And I'm one of them." The man nodded toward a bottle of wine passing by on a serving tray. "Two weeks ago, I bought Richardson Vineyards, lock, stock and barrel. Your next delivery will bear the new label. I just thought I should introduce myself and give you all a heads-up."

"I hadn't heard." Cole still regarded the man suspiciously. "Congrats on acquiring the vineyard, Mr. Valentine. I'll let my mother know—"

"Actually, I was hoping to meet your family. Especially your grandfather, Joseph." The man looked less cocky. There was a hint of discomfort in his dark eyes as they scanned the room.

"And why is that, Mr. Valentine?" Cole asked again.

"I suppose there is no delicate way to say this." The man sighed heavily, then straightened his tie. He glanced around the space surreptitiously. "I'm his… brother."

"My grandfather is an only child. Just like my father." Cole stood taller, clenching his jaw.

He had no idea what kind of game this man was running, but he would gladly escort his happy ass to the door. There was no way he'd let this man ruin his mother's special night.

"Joseph was his mother's only child," the man clarified. "But not our father's. And thanks to you and the ancestry registry you joined, I finally know who my real father was—your great-grandfather King Abbott. That makes me your grandfather's half brother."

Cole and Ren looked at each other. Her eyes went wide, and his heart was racing.

Shit.

Three months ago, Renee had decided to join an ancestry registry to try to locate Wilhelmina's daughter. Cole had always thought it would be cool and interesting to learn more about his family roots, so he'd joined the registry, too. He'd never imagined that *he'd* be the one to find a long-lost relative.

"Hey, don't I know you?" Cole's grandfather walked over, a glass of bourbon in his hand as he rubbed his chin and tried to place the man.

"Hello, Joseph." The man held out his hand, which trembled slightly.

"So I do know you!" Gramps said, narrowing his gaze as he shook it. "Now don't tell me. Just give me a minute to place you."

"Pops," Cole said gently. "This man…Abbott Valentine…he says he's your—"

"Brother," the man said, still clutching Joseph's hand. "I'm your half brother. And I could really use your help."

* * * * *

Discover the Valentines,
the long-lost relatives of
the Bourbon Brothers, in
Reese Ryan's new series,
Valentine Vineyards,
coming soon from Harlequin Desire.

And don't miss
a single Bourbon Brothers novel
by Reese Ryan!

Savannah's Secrets
The Billionaire's Legacy
Engaging the Enemy
A Reunion of Rivals
Waking Up Married
The Bad Boy Experiment

Exclusively from Harlequin Desire.

COMING NEXT MONTH FROM

HARLEQUIN DESIRE

#2851 RANCHER'S FORGOTTEN RIVAL

The Carsons of Lone Rock • by Maisey Yates

No one infuriates Juniper Sohappy more than ranch owner Chance Carson. But when Juniper finds him injured and with amnesia on her property, she must help. He believes he's her ranch hand, and unexpected passion flares. But when the truth comes to light, will everything fall apart?

#2852 FROM FEUDING TO FALLING

Texas Cattleman's Club: Fathers and Sons • by Jules Bennett

When Carson Wentworth wins the TCC presidency, tensions flare between him and rival Lana Langley. But to end their familiy feud and secure a fortune for the club, Carson needs her—as his fake fiancée. If they can only ignore the heat between them...

#2853 A SONG OF SECRETS

Hana Trio • by Jayci Lee

After their breakup a decade ago, cellist Angie Han needs composer Jonathan Shin's song to save her family's organization. Striking an uneasy truce, they find their attraction still sizzles. But as their connection grows, will past secrets ruin everything?

#2854 MIDNIGHT SON

Gambling Men • by Barbara Dunlop

Determined to protect his mentor, ruggedly handsome Alaskan businessman Nathaniel Stone is suspicious of the woman claiming to be his boss's long-lost daughter, Sophie Crush. He agrees to get close to her to uncover her intentions, but he cannot ignore their undeniable attraction...

#2855 MILLION-DOLLAR MIX-UP

The Dunn Brothers • by Jessica Lemmon

With her only client MIA, talent agent Kendall Squire travels to his twin's luxe mountain cabin to ask him to fill in. But Max Dunn left Hollywood behind. Now, as they're trapped by a blizzard, things unexpectedly heat up. Has Kendall found her leading man?

#2856 THE PROBLEM WITH PLAYBOYS

Little Black Book of Secrets • by Karen Booth

Publicist Chloe Burnett is a fixer, and sports agent Parker Sullivan needs her to take down a vicious gossip account. She never mixes business with pleasure, but the playboy's hard to resist. When they find themselves in the account's crosshairs, can their relationship survive?

SPECIAL EXCERPT FROM

DESIRE

Eve Martin has one goal—find her nephew's father—and her unlikely ally is hotelier Rafael Wentworth, who's just returned to Texas and the family who abandoned him. Soon, she's falling hard for the playboy despite their differences...and their secrets.

Read on for a sneak peek at The Rebel's Return, *by Nadine Gonzalez.*

"I'm opening a guesthouse in town, similar to this, but better."

"You're here to check out the competition, aren't you?"

Rafael raised a finger to his lips. "Shh."

"That's sneaky," Eve said with a little smile. "I knew you had a motive for coming here."

He winked. "Just not the motive you thought."

She responded with a roll of the eyes. He noticed her long lashes fanned the high slopes of her cheeks. In the intimate light of the inn's lobby, her skin was smoother than he could have ever imagined.

Rafael was glad the tension that had built up in the car was subsiding. He wanted to make her laugh again, the way she'd laughed when they were alone in the garden. Her laughter had leaped out as if springing from a sealed cave. He'd wanted to take her in his arms and hold her close until she settled down.

"Incoming!"

Lost in the fantasy of holding her, he didn't quite understand what she was saying. "What's that?"

"Just...shut up."

She stepped up to him and brushed her lips to his in a whisper of a kiss. Rafael tensed, the muscles of his abdomen tightening. "Act like you're into it," she murmured through clenched teeth. With every nerve ending in his body setting off sparks, he didn't have to

HDEXP0122A

rely on dormant acting skills. He gripped her waist, pulled her close and kissed her hard, deep and slow. She gripped the lapel of his suit jacket and opened to his kiss. He heard her groan just before she tore herself away.

"I think we're good," she said, her voice shaky.

He was shaken, too. "How the hell do you figure?"

"I kissed you to create a distraction," she said. "P&J just walked in."

Paul and Jennifer Carlton were the most annoying couple in Texas, but at this moment he was making plans to send them a fruit basket and a bottle of wine.

"Here I thought you wanted to test that 'sex in an inn' theory."

"Stop thinking that," she scolded. "They're right over there. Don't look now, though."

He wouldn't dream of it. Her swollen lips had his undivided attention.

"Okay… They've entered the dining hall. You can look now."

"Nah. I'll take your word for it."

The manager returned with the keys to their suite, the one with the two distinct and separate bedrooms. The man was a little red in the face from what he'd undoubtedly witnessed.

Rafael plucked the key cards from his hand. "I'll take those. Thanks."

"Anything else, sir?"

"Send up laundry services, will you?" Rafael said. "And your best bottle of tequila."

The manager cleared his throat. "Certainly, sir. Enjoy your evening."

Don't miss what happens next in
The Rebel's Return *by Nadine Gonzalez,*
the next book in the Texas Cattleman's Club:
Fathers and Sons series!

Available February 2022 wherever
Harlequin Desire books and ebooks are sold.

Harlequin.com

HDEXP0122A

SPECIAL EXCERPT FROM

You won't want to miss
The True Cowboy of Sunset Ridge,
***the thrilling final installment of* New York Times**
bestselling author Maisey Yates's Gold Valley series!

Bull rider Colt Daniels has a wild reputation, but after losing his friend on the rodeo circuit, he's left it all behind. If only he could walk away from the temptation of Mallory Chance so easily. He can't offer her the future she deserves, but when he ends up caring for his friend's tiny baby, he needs Mallory's help. But is it temporary or their chance at a forever family?

"It's you, isn't it?"

She turned, and there he was.

So close.

Impossibly close.

And she didn't know if she could survive it.

Because those electric blue eyes were looking right into hers. But this time, it wasn't from across a crowded bar. It was right there.

Right there.

And she didn't have a deadweight clinging to her side that kept her from going where she wanted to go, doing what she wanted to do. She was free. Unencumbered, for the first time in fifteen years. For the first damn time.

She was standing there, and she was just Mallory.

Jared wasn't there. Griffin wasn't there. Her parents weren't there.

She was standing on her own, standing there with no one and nothing to tell her what to do, no one and nothing to make her feel a certain thing.

So it was all just him. Blinding electric blue, brilliant and scalding.

Perfect.

"I...I think so. Unless...unless you think I'm someone else." It was much less confident and witty than she'd intended. But she didn't feel capable of witty just now.

"You were here once. About six months ago."

He remembered her. He remembered her. This man who had haunted her dreams—no, not haunted, created them—who had filled her mind with erotic imagery that had never existed there before, was…talking about her. He was.

He thought of her. He remembered her.

"I was," she said.

He looked behind her, then back at her. "Where's the boyfriend?"

He asked the question with an edge of hostility. It made her shiver.

"Not here."

"Good." His lips tipped upward into a smile.

"I…" She didn't know what to say. She didn't know what to say because this shimmering feeling inside her was clearly, clearly shared and…

Suddenly her freedom felt terrifying. That freedom that had felt, only a moment before, exhilarating suddenly felt like too much. She wanted to hide. Wanted to scamper under the bar and get behind the bar stool so that she could put something between herself and this electric man. She wondered if she was ready for this.

Because there was no question what this was.

One night.

With nothing at all between them. Nothing but unfamiliar motel bedsheets. A bed she'd never sleep in again and a man she would never sleep with again.

She understood that.